HER FESTIVE
FLIRTATION

HER FESTIVE
FLIRTATION

THERESE BEHARRIE

MILLS & BOON

First published in Great Britain 2018
by Mills & Boon, an imprint of HarperCollins*Publishers*
1 London Bridge Street, London, SE1 9GF

Large Print edition 2019

© 2018 Therese Beharrie

ISBN: 978-0-263-08214-2

MIX
Paper from
responsible sources
FSC™ C007454

This book is produced from independently certified
FSC™ paper to ensure responsible forest management. For
more information visit www.harpercollins.co.uk/green.

Printed and bound in Great Britain
by CPI Group (UK) Ltd, Croydon, CR0 4YY

For Grant, who makes every Christmas the best day of the year.

And for my family. I love you.

CHAPTER ONE

'MA'AM, I CAN'T LET you go in there.'

'But—'

'No "buts".' The man turned back to where smoke obscured the eco-estate where Ava Keller's home was. 'There's no way you're going into that.'

Ava gritted her teeth. She hated him. Though she'd never met the man before, she hated him.

The rational voice in her head told her she was projecting. That coming home from work to find her home covered in smoke had upset her. That being upset had manifested itself in her short tone and strong emotions. Like hatred.

Yes, the rational voice said. She was definitely projecting. But then, she'd never prized rationality in stressful situations. That was why, when she'd been left at the altar a year before, she'd attended the wedding reception. She'd eaten the cake. She'd gone on her honeymoon.

Rationality wouldn't make her feel less stressed. Nor would it make her less emotional. And rationality wasn't going to save one of the only things in her life that was still important to her.

So when an idea occurred to her and the rational voice warned against it, she knew she was going to do it. And though it was a bad idea—a *terrible* one—she would do it anyway.

Heaven help her.

She turned, walked a few steps away from the wall of men blocking the path to her house, and let out a bloodcurdling scream.

They hurried towards her, and later she would think that they must have made quite a picture. Those huge, muscular men in their official uniforms—some firefighters, some police—hurrying over to her as if they were lions and she were fresh meat.

She would also later think that at least ten men hurrying over to her had been overkill. But right now she was pretending to be a damsel in distress, and she was certain that merely the *idea* of that caused men to flock.

Really, her duping them was their own fault. *And* that of her excellent acting skills.

Unfortunately, being a copywriter for a cybersecurity company didn't often allow her to illustrate how dramatic she could be.

'I think… I think I just saw a *person*.' She gripped the shirt of the man closest to her. 'Right there—down the path at that bush.' Now she injected a layer of panic into her voice. 'It's so close to the fire, Sergeant. And it looked like my neighbour. An old man with no teeth.'

There was a beat when she wondered whether she'd gone too far. She *had* laid it on a little thick. Mr Kinney was barely fifty. He had all his teeth and he wasn't in danger.

To make it more believable, she let out another tiny little screech. And when the man who'd blocked her from getting near her house moved forward to comfort her she cried, 'No, no, not me. Help *him. Help him!*'

If the fire didn't do the job first, Ava knew she was going to burn in hell.

But it worked, and three of the men ran down the pathway while the others moved forward, bodies tensed, ready to help if necessary.

It was all she needed. Without a second thought for how irrational she was acting, Ava bolted up the incline of the road she'd been blocked from earlier, and didn't stop until she was so far from the men she'd left behind she could barely see them.

Nor could she see in front of her.

When panic crept up her throat, she ignored it. Told herself to remember all those nights she'd spent unable to sleep and Zorro had comforted her. To remember that it was only when she was looking after him that she felt capable. Able. And not as if some of her personality traits—her honesty, her bluntness—meant she somehow couldn't be a partner. A *wife*.

But all thought fled from her mind as her body adjusted to its new environment. The smoke seemed to be stuck in her mouth. Clogging her lungs. Burning her eyes. She pulled off her shirt and tied it around her nose and mouth, trying to keep her eyes open.

It didn't make much difference. The smoke was so thick she could barely see her hands in front of her. And the more she tried, the more her eyes burned.

So she wasn't entirely surprised when she walked right into a wall.

The force of it stunned her. But after a moment she realised it wasn't a wall. Not unless this wall had suddenly grown hands and gripped her arms to keep her from falling.

She was pretty sure she'd walked into a human. A human *man*.

As opposed to an alien man?

Clearly the smoke was doing more damage than she'd thought.

She heard a muffled sound coming from the man. He was obviously trying to tell her something, but he was wearing a firefighter's mask and she couldn't make out a single word. She shook her head and then, deciding that this interaction was taking precious time from her rescue mission, she pushed past him.

But she'd forgotten he had his hands on her arms, and they tightened on her before she could move.

'What are you *doing*?' the man asked now, wrenching off his mask.

She still couldn't see him. Which, she thought, was probably a good thing, since his voice didn't indicate that he felt any positive emotion towards her.

'I have to get to my house.'

'Ma'am, this area has been evacuated. The fire could reach us at any moment.'

'So why aren't you out there, making sure that it doesn't?'

'Are you serious?' The disbelief in his tone made his voice sound familiar. 'You *have* to leave, ma'am. Your property is not as important as your life. Or mine.'

'It isn't about my *property*,' she said, her

voice hoarse from smoke and desperation. 'My cat is in there. I have to… I have to save him.'

Something pulsed in the air after she'd finished talking, and she could have sworn she'd heard him curse.

'Where's your house?'

Stunned, she took a moment to respond. 'It's not far from here. I can show you.'

'No. Just tell me the number and I'll make sure I find the damn cat.'

'Seventeen.' She hesitated when he handed her his mask and turned away. 'Wait! Don't *you* need this?'

'Yes,' he ground out. 'But you're going to need it more. Just put it on and go back to where you came from. I'll find you.'

It was a few seconds before she realised he wasn't there any more.

'Check under the bed!' she shouted at her loudest, and then she put the mask on and retraced her steps back towards the men—no easy feat with the smoke even thicker now.

She was immediately swarmed, but she ignored them—ignored the complaints and chastisement—and kept her eyes on the clouds of smoke in front of her.

She only realised she hadn't taken off the mask when someone gently removed it from her. A paramedic, she thought, as it was replaced by an oxygen mask and she was asked to breathe in and out as the woman listened to her heartbeat before gently checking her body for burns.

Rationality won out now. It reminded Ava that she'd put her life in danger. That she'd put someone else's life in danger, too. And, even though the thought of losing Zorro sent pangs of pain through her body, she couldn't justify that.

So when the paramedic told her she needed to sit down, to drink some water, to get her heart-rate down, she obeyed, not voicing any of the protests screaming through her head.

A cat. *A freaking cat.*

That was what he was risking his life for. That was what he was abandoning all the rules of his training for. He could see the headlines now: *Volunteer firefighter Noah Giles dies trying to save a cat.* Smoke blurred his eyes, grated in his throat, his lungs, but somehow he made it to number seventeen. Smoke shrouded it, much as it did the other houses on the estate. When he'd been making his final rounds, checking that humans and pets had been evacuated, he hadn't expected to find anyone.

They'd had the entire day to evacuate the area, and it had been erring on the side of caution, really, just in case the veld fire should spread.

Except now he wasn't being cautious, he thought, coughing as he pushed open the door—in any other circumstance, he'd probably be annoyed that it had been left unlocked—and leaned against the wall. His head felt light, and it was pure determination that pushed him forward.

Determination spurred on by the emotion in the woman's voice when she'd told him about the cat. It had been familiar, somehow, and had hit him in a place he hadn't known existed. As if he cared that someone loved a cat as much as this woman loved hers.

And since he was risking his life for this cat, clearly he *did* care.

The damn cat had better be the most intelligent cat in the entire world, he thought. He'd be pretty annoyed if he died for any other kind. Just before Christmas, too, when he was planning to tell his father that after seven years of restlessness he was finally ready to put down some roots.

But only in terms of where you live.

He grunted. Then chose to ignore the unhelpful voice in his head and focused on checking the entire house systematically. Being inside protected him from the smoke somewhat, but he knew he couldn't stick around for long.

When he got to the bedroom, something told him to look under the bed. Beady eyes stared back at him when he did so, and air gushed from his lungs. How could he be this relieved at finding a pet that wasn't even his own? He shook his head, refusing to think about it, and then belly-crawled under the bed and gently pulled the cat into his arms.

It gave a low *meow*—a warning, he thought— but he didn't pay much attention to it. His goal now was to get back to safety.

He was already back at the front door before he realised he couldn't let the cat go out into the smoke. And shortly afterwards he realised the same thing about himself.

He knew that the cat—which was already wriggling in his arms—would run away the second he put him down. And so, taking a deep breath—and once again rethinking all his decisions in life—Noah stuffed the cat inside his open jacket before buttoning it up.

There was some struggling—and a sharp

pain as the cat's claws stuck into his belly—but eventually the cat stilled. He looked around for something he could use to cover his face before he braved the smoke again, but instead his eyes rested on a picture that stood on the mantelpiece. A picture of all the people he'd cared about growing up.

And among all their faces, his own.

If she'd ever wanted to discover how to upset a paramedic, she'd found out that evening.

'You *have* to go to the hospital.'

'No.'

'Ma'am—' The woman cut herself off and hissed out a breath. 'Look, your heart rate is still high, and one of the things that can happen with smoke inhalation is—'

'Cardiac arrest. Yeah, I know. I watched that TV show, too.'

'It's not from a *show.*' The paramedic wasn't even trying to hide her annoyance now. 'I'm a medical professional and I know that—'

Ava didn't hear the rest of the woman's speech. She'd stopped listening the moment she saw a man emerge from the smoke. Ignoring the now protesting woman, she stood and pushed forward.

And then stopped when she saw who the man was.

'Noah?'

She watched as he tossed aside a cloth—no, not a cloth; the throw that had once been over her couch—and then bend over and brace himself on his knees.

'Hey, paramedic lady!' Ava said, turning around in panic. But the woman was way ahead of her, and brushed past Ava with the oxygen mask and tank Ava had been using minutes before.

Just as they had with her, the men rallied around Noah. Though this time, of course, it was because Noah was their colleague, and not some foolish woman who'd run into the line of fire—literally—to save a cat.

She watched helplessly as they guided Noah towards the ambulance, and then, when they were there, tried to get him out of his suit. But he shook his head and made eye contact with her.

It jolted her heart. Had the poor thing sprinting as if it were in a life-and-death race it *had* to win.

So, nothing's changed in the seven years since you've seen him, then?

Clearing her throat—her mind—she took

a step forward, her legs shaking though her strides were steady.

When she reached him, he pulled the oxygen mask from his face, coughed, and then said, 'Are we going to have to talk about why you decided to run into a fire to rescue a cat, Avalanche?'

His words were said with a crooked half-smile, and then he began to unbutton the jacket she'd only just noticed was moving to reveal a squirming Zorro.

There had been a pause before she'd even realised it was her cat. And that pause came because she'd been distracted by the muscular chest under the white vest Noah had just uncovered.

No, she thought. It had been *years* since she'd seen Noah. *Years* since she'd even thought about the silly crush she'd had on her brother's best friend. Or about the kisses they'd once shared.

There was no way any remnants of that crush were still there. She'd been in a five-year relationship since then. She'd almost got married.

But you didn't *get married*, a voice in her head said enticingly.

So clearly, there *was* a way.

CHAPTER TWO

AVA REACHED OVER and pulled the cat into her arms. Noah noted the squirming stopped immediately. *Go figure.*

'No one calls me Avalanche any more.'

It was exactly the kind of thing he'd expected her to say. And even though he didn't know what to do about the nostalgia surging in his chest, he smiled.

'You used to love it.'

'I *never* loved it.'

'Why would I keep calling you that if you didn't love it?'

'I've asked myself that question for most of my life.'

He smirked. Then heard the next words come out of his mouth before he could stop them. 'I've missed you, Avalanche.'

Her eyes softened, and she reached out and placed the oxygen mask back over his nose and mouth. 'It's nice to see you, too, Noah—'

Her voice broke and he frowned, pulling the mask away again.

'Has someone checked you out?'

'I'm fine.'

'I told her she needed to go to the hospital,' said the paramedic he hadn't even realised was still there. 'But she doesn't believe me.'

'Why? What's wrong?'

'Nothing,' Ava said with a roll of her eyes. 'I'm fine.'

'Elevated heart rate,' the paramedic told him.

'She's at risk for cardiac arrest?'

'I am a healthy twenty-five-year-old,' Ava interrupted as the paramedic was about to give an answer. 'I have a healthy heart. In fact, I had a check-up at the doctor's last week and she confirmed it.'

Twenty-five. The last time he'd seen her she'd been eighteen. A kid, really. *Not that that stopped you from treating her like a woman.*

He clenched his jaw. Told himself to ignore the unwelcome voice in his head. But when his eyes moved over her—when they told him she was very much a woman now—the memories that voice evoked became a hell of a lot harder to ignore.

He shook his head. 'Smoke inhalation is dangerous.'

'Which is why *you* should be going to the hospital and not me. I was in there a fraction of the time you were.'

'But my heart rate is okay.' The paramedic nodded when he looked over, and he gave Ava a winning smile. 'See?'

'Smoke inhalation is dangerous,' she replied thinly, with a smile of her own, though hers was remarkably more fake than his.

It made nostalgia pulse again, but memories of the way things had been before he'd left made him wonder if nostalgia was really what he was feeling.

But she was right about the smoke inhalation, and because of it—and because he knew his team wouldn't let him work unless he got checked out—he agreed.

'Fine. But if I'm going, you're going, too.'

She opened her mouth, but he shot her a look and she nodded.

'Okay. But we're stopping at the veterinary hospital first. I need to make sure Zorro's okay.'

The fierceness of her voice softened as she said the cat's name, and he watched as she pressed a kiss into its fur. It stumped him— one, that she could show more affection to a cat than she could to a man she'd basically grown up with and, two, that she could show affection to *that* cat.

It was the ugliest cat he'd ever seen.

He assumed Ava had named him Zorro because of the black, almost mask-like patches on his face. And he supposed in some way those patches *were* cute. But he couldn't say the same for the rest of the cat's body. The orange, brown and white splotches looked as if the cat was the result of a scientific experiment gone wrong.

He'd never really been one for cats, and perhaps he was just biased against them. But, he thought, eyeing the cat again, he didn't think so.

He would never have said the cat was ugly as he looked at Ava, though. Her brown eyes were filled with emotion—love, affection, he couldn't quite tell—and her tall frame had relaxed.

And he realised that if he wanted her to get checked out he was going to have to agree to take the ugly cat to the veterinary hospital.

'He's sitting in the back.'

Five hours later they'd both been checked out. Noah had been put on oxygen for a portion of that time, while they ran tests, and when he'd met Ava in the waiting room later she'd told him the same thing had happened with her.

Though the test results had shown nothing alarming, they'd been given strict instructions to rest, and to return if any potentially danger-ous symptoms emerged.

'You didn't have to wait for me,' Noah told her as she got up and joined him.

'I know. But I… I wanted to know that you were okay.' She ran a hand over the curls at the top of her head. 'I'm pretty sure Jaden would kill me if I were responsible for the death of his best man.'

'That's all I am to you?' he teased, though it came out a little more seriously than he'd in-tended.

'No, of course not.' She paused. 'You're also my only way to call the vet and ask about Zorro. My phone's died.'

He laughed, and it turned into a cough.

'You're sure you're okay?'

'Fine.' He waved a hand. 'Just normal after-effects.'

She bit her lip. 'I really am sorry. I didn't mean for you to get dragged into this.'

'I'm glad I was the one who *did* get dragged into it,' he retorted. 'At least I have training.'

'Ah, yes—one of the thousands of things you can do when you have family money.'

He winced. 'How did you go from apologising to insulting me?'

She grinned, and his mind scrambled to figure out why his body was responding. He'd given himself a stern talking-to when he'd left all those years ago. Hadn't spoken to Ava since then. His body had no business reacting to her smile.

'It's one of my unique talents.'

What are the others?

Now his mind froze, and when Ava didn't say anything else, he wondered whether he'd said it out loud. But her expression didn't change, and he put down the strange thought to the after-effects of inhaling smoke. There could be no other explanation.

Sure, keep telling yourself that.

'So, can I call the vet?' she asked after a moment.

He blinked, then handed her his phone and took the seat she'd vacated as she made the call.

He watched as she spoke to the vet. Watched as she set a hand on her hip and then lifted it, toying with her curls again. She'd cut her hair into a tapered style that somehow made the oval shape of her face seem both classic and modern.

He supposed those terms would work to describe her entire appearance. He'd always thought her beautiful—with an innocent kind of beauty that was much too pure for him—but with the haircut, and the clothes she wore that suited that cut, she *was* an enticing mix of classic and modern that made him want—

He stopped himself. Frowned at the direction of his thoughts. He couldn't think of his best friend's kid sister as *enticing*. He couldn't think about wanting anything when it came to her.

She was just Ava. Little Avalanche. The girl who'd run in circles around him just for the fun of it when she was six. Who'd snorted if she laughed hard enough up until she was fourteen. Who'd asked him to be her first kiss so she could practise, and who'd eagerly responded when he'd kissed her a second time—

Nope. *No.* That line of thinking was going to get him nowhere.

But when she turned and smiled at him—and his body yearned to get *somewhere*—he realised that Jaden's wedding was going to be more complicated than he'd expected.

CHAPTER THREE

HE HADN'T CHANGED one bit.

No, Ava thought as Noah stood, her eyes flitting over him. He *had* changed. Though she now remembered how greedily she'd taken in his muscles earlier, she'd forgotten about them between then and now.

Possibly because he was wearing one of his colleague's ill-fitting T-shirts.

Probably because she'd been too distracted by his face.

It had happened before, too many times to count. And Ava didn't even blame herself for it. How could she? Objectively, Noah had the prettiest face she'd ever seen. And though the word didn't seem to fit with the rest of him— not any more, since the strong, muscular body he had now was more rugged than the lithe one he'd had when they were younger—she couldn't deny the perfect lines and angles of his face *were* pretty.

But just because she couldn't blame herself

for it didn't mean she didn't find it annoying. It was. Because if he hadn't been so pretty she might not have found herself *still* having this absurd crush. *Years* later.

And then he walked towards her, rubbed a hand down her arm, and said something in that deliciously deep voice of his. And the voice in her head that had called her a liar when she'd put her crush down to just his looks laughed and laughed.

Damn it.

'Avalanche?'

'Hmm?' She shook her head. 'Oh. You said something?' If only she could remember what.

'Yes.'

'Yes?' His hand dropped. 'What do you mean, *yes*?'

Double damn it. Clearly her guess had been wrong.

'I mean, yes—' She exhaled sharply when she couldn't think of an appropriate cover-up. 'Yes, I have no idea what you said and my attempt at hiding it has failed miserably.'

He stared at her, and then he laughed. 'Clearly you're the same old Ava. Honest even when it doesn't benefit you.'

'Would it kill you to not be so blunt? No one needs you to be this honest.'

'Yes, that's me,' she said brightly, hoping it would banish the darkness of Milo's voice in her head. The memories that voice inevitably evoked. The pretence of the rest of her wedding day. The weeks after, when she'd looked in the mirror and asked herself why she couldn't be different. Better. *Easier.* 'Would you repeat what you said?'

'I asked where you'll be staying tonight?'

'Jaden's,' she said automatically. But then she shook her head. 'No, Jaden isn't here. He and Leela are staying over at the vineyard their wedding is going to be at. They want a better idea of what their wedding will feel like.' She rolled her eyes. 'As if it will change anything. The wedding's two weeks away. What are they going to do if it doesn't "feel" right?' She sighed. 'I guess I'll be staying at a hotel.'

'Why not your mom and dad's?'

'They're with Jaden and Leela at the wedding venue.'

'Sounds horrific.'

'Yes,' she agreed with a small smile. 'I can't imagine anything worse than a wedding at Christmastime.'

She knew that because *her* wedding had been at Christmastime. And not only had her day been spoiled, but her entire festive season. She was still not prepared to spend the first anniversary of her being jilted at another wedding. With the same guests. And the same whispers.

But she had no choice. Her brother was getting married.

'Of course, the fact that this isn't exactly a romantic weekend for Jaden and Leela sucks, too. My parents and Leela's parents are there, so Jaden and Leela probably had to get separate bedrooms.'

It hadn't occurred to her before, but it amused her now.

'Oh, no,' Noah said with a frown. 'Your parents can't think—?' He broke off when she gave him a look. 'Apparently they can.'

'Unfortunately, my parents can and will believe whatever they want of their children.'

Like the way they thought the collapse of Ava's wedding had been because of Milo's faults and not Ava's. And how they still didn't see anything wrong with how grumpy she was—or wonder how much easier she could have been—even after a broken engagement.

'Anyway,' she continued, 'no one's there. And my access to all those places are locked in the drawer next to my bed.' She closed her eyes briefly. 'So, yes, a hotel.'

'What about Zorro?'

She lifted a brow. 'Are you still looking out for him?'

'I'm looking out for *you.*'

She thought she saw him hesitate before he continued.

'You're my best friend's sister. There's an unspoken moral code that requires me to help you when your brother can't.'

'I'd like to think that moral code comes from the fact that you and I were friends once, too,' she said slowly. 'It doesn't matter anyway,' she added, when the thought had her stomach twisting. 'The vet wants to keep Zorro overnight. He wants to make sure he's okay.'

'Are you okay with that?'

'Of course I am.'

'Sure,' he said easily. 'So there's no part of you that's worried about him?'

When her spoken agreement got caught by the emotion in her throat, she sighed. 'There's a *big* part of me that's worried about him. But he's in the best place to make sure he's okay.'

He studied her. 'He'll be okay,' he said quietly, and then, as if he understood that she wouldn't be able to hold back the tears if they kept on talking about it, he said, 'You should stay with me.'

She stared him. 'What?'

'You should stay with me,' he said again. 'At my place.'

'What place? Your dad's?'

'I'm a big boy, Ava,' he said dryly. 'I have a place of my own.'

'I meant,' she said deliberately, when his words sent thrills down her spine, 'that you've been away for seven years. How do you have a place of your own?'

'I invested in property.'

'Of course you did,' she muttered. 'No, thanks, Noah. I think I'll just get a hotel room.'

'You don't know how long it'll be before you'll be able to go home.' He paused. 'You might have to spend a couple of nights there.'

'I'll survive.'

'What about Zorro?'

She narrowed her eyes. 'I told you—'

'Yes, he's staying at the vet's tonight. But what happens tomorrow, when they call you to tell you he's fine? That he can come home?'

'I'm sure I'll be back in my own house by then.'

'But what if you're not?' He waited a beat. 'I have a pet-friendly home.'

'Noah—'

'Ava.'

Their gazes locked. Her brain said, *No, Ava*; her body said, *Yes, please*. The juxtaposition fluttered on her skin, and she blamed her gooseflesh on that and not on how sexy and serious Noah's eyes looked. Or on the memory of how that was exactly how they'd looked before he'd kissed her all those years ago...

'No, Noah.'

She said it with a sigh of regret. She hoped he wouldn't hear that, but her filter wasn't working properly. She was too tired. Her throat ached. Her lungs pained. Her body reminded her that she'd done a full day of work before she'd arrived home to find the place full of smoke. Not to mention the swirling in her head at the unwelcome feelings and memories being in Noah's presence evoked.

'I've already put you out way too much tonight. I'm the reason you're here. You should go home by yourself—' Had she *really* just said that? '—and get some rest. Besides, I have to call my family now, before they hear about the evacuation, freak out and start driving back here in the middle of the night. And I do *not* want to tell them—specifically, Jaden—that I'm staying at your place tonight.'

'Ava...' he said softly, and walked closer to her.

Something pressed into the backs of her legs, and she realised it was one of the seats in the waiting room. Because when he'd moved closer to her she'd moved back.

Stay.

She straightened. 'Noah—'

'Let me speak,' he interrupted, and the tone of his voice—seductive, commanding—silenced her. 'It's been a difficult night. We're both exhausted, and it's going to take more energy than either of us has to find you a hotel. I'm not leaving you alone to arrange all this,' he said when she opened her mouth. 'And I'm not even mentioning clean clothes, proper toiletries, a warm meal. Stay with me.'

'What do I tell my family?'

'Whatever you like. It's the easiest option,' he said with a smile, as if he knew she was already starting to formulate the lie she was going to tell them. 'You'd do the same thing for me, Ava. We're family, too.'

She nearly laughed. 'I haven't seen you in seven years, Noah.'

'Doesn't change anything.' He paused. 'I've only seen Jaden three times during those seven years. All three times it was because he'd come to see me. Because he considered me to be family.'

'You're his best friend.'

'Family,' he said firmly. 'Friends come and go. And I went. If we weren't family I wouldn't be back here at Christmas, preparing to be best man at your brother's wedding.'

'You're...stubborn,' she said, when defeat washed over her.

'I like to think of it as persistent.'

'Well, you better hope persistence will help us if Jaden ever discovers the truth about the lie I'm about to tell him and our parents.'

'Noah, you know I appreciate you offering me a place to stay, but—' Ava broke off, wondering how to tell him. But then she remembered that he already knew she was honest. 'But it looks like Father Christmas and the elves threw up in here.'

Noah chuckled. 'That's not a bad description, actually.'

He stood next to her and she held her breath, as if somehow it would make her less aware of him.

'I had a company come in and decorate for Christmas before I got here. They got a bit... carried away.'

She took in the tinsel that hung on every flat surface, the Christmas stockings that accompanied it. The Christmas lights that were draped around pieces of furniture that should not have lights around them. And, of course, the gigantic Christmas tree next to the fireplace.

'I think that's an understatement.'

'Probably.'

He took the handbag and coat that been draped over her shoulder and arm respectively, and hung them on a coat rack she hadn't noticed.

'I've been meaning to do something to make it less...*this*—' he nodded his head at the decorations '—but I haven't had the time.'

'Christmas season is fire season in Cape Town.'

'Yeah. And this season's been particularly bad. Hence the fact that I—a mere volunteer—have been fighting fires for pretty much the entire two weeks since I've been here.'

She took a seat at the counter in his kitchen, accepting the glass of water he offered her. 'Is that why I didn't even know you were back here?'

'I told Jaden. It must have slipped his mind.'

'Must have,' she said softly.

But she didn't think that was it. Jaden hadn't been entirely forthcoming with her since he and his fiancée had announced that their wedding would be at the same time of year hers had been, almost one year later to the day. In fact, he was avoiding her. More so since Leela had asked her to be a bridesmaid.

So she would put down Jaden's neglect in telling her Noah was back to that, and not to the fact that he hadn't wanted her to know. Things had moved on since Jaden had caught them kissing that one time. It probably had nothing to do with the anger he'd felt towards both of them back then.

Probably.

'You okay?'

She looked up to see Noah's eyes steady on her. 'Perfect. This place is amazing.'

She looked around at the light green walls, the large windows that offered an incredible view of the mountains and the hills, the stone-coloured furniture. She took in the marble countertops, the sleek, top-of-the-line appliances, the white and yellow palette that brightened the kitchen.

And then her eyes rested on the sexy man who looked so at home in all of it. And although her heart did unwanted cartwheels in her chest, she forced calm into her voice.

'I mean, what I can actually see underneath all this tinsel is amazing.'

'Oh, ha-ha.'

She grinned. 'So, how about you show me to the shower, Mr Festive?'

CHAPTER FOUR

WHEN HE'D STUDIED photography after school it had been because he'd had a passion for it. He'd enjoyed the challenge of seeing things in new ways. In ways others didn't. He'd created a website to show off his work, and when he'd received that first enquiry to use one of his pictures he'd realised he could use his passion to make money.

Soon his photos had garnered more attention. And then a photo editor for a popular nature magazine had reached out to him about a job in Namibia. And suddenly he'd realised he could use his passion to give in to his wanderlust.

He supposed his surname had given him a push that most twenty-year-olds didn't get. The Giles name was still synonymous with the media empire his great-great-uncle had created. The empire that had been passed down to his grandfather, when his great-great-uncle had died childless, and then down to his father.

Having an empire and money behind him

had meant he could take only the jobs that interested him. That he'd been able to use his skill and passion for jobs that *meant* something to the world. That he'd been able to use the money he didn't need to invest in properties back home in South Africa and wherever else his heart desired.

All while avoiding the pitfalls of settling down. The trap he'd seen his father fall into over and over again since his mother had died. But he couldn't deny that it felt good to have a place of his own. Not somewhere he just stayed, but somewhere he *lived*.

He'd only been back in Cape Town for a fortnight, but it was a source of pride for him. And never more than at this moment, as he showed Ava to his spare bedroom.

When she'd disappeared into the bathroom he went to his own room and put some of the spare clothing he had there in hers. And then he went back to the kitchen, to start on the meal he'd promised her. Which, he thought even before he reached the kitchen, was a stupid idea. On his best days he could manage to fry an egg. And it would usually end up deformed. Edible, but deformed.

It would definitely not be the kind of warm

meal he'd promised Ava, so he called the twenty-four-hour deli up the road. He was almost out through the door to go and fetch the food, too, before he realised he looked like crap. He'd changed out of his firefighter's uniform before going to the hospital, but he was still sweaty and grimy. And fairly certain he would not have wanted to meet himself, let alone hand over food to someone looking like he did at that moment.

He went to his room, threw off his clothes and headed to the shower. He heaved a sigh when the water hit his body. It kneaded muscles he hadn't realised were tight and painful. It also reminded him that he'd stuffed a cat into his jacket and the cat had *not* appreciated it.

He washed his hair, his body and then, feeling faintly human again, put on clean clothes. But before he put on his top he realised he should probably put something on the scratches on his stomach. They were deeper than he'd first realised. So he grabbed his top, heading to the kitchen where he kept the first-aid kit.

'I thought they fixed everything at the hospital.'

He was halfway through putting salve on the scratches when she spoke. He glanced back, and his throat dried when he saw her in his clothes.

They were too big for her, but they looked better on her than they ever had on him.

'Uh...they did. But they also took me at my word when I told them I had no external injuries. I forgot about these.'

She walked around the counter and he got a whiff of the fruity scent of the shower gel he'd put in his spare bathroom. It smelled a hell of a lot sexier on her than it did in the bottle.

Oh, boy.

'Which external injuries?' she said, and then, though he tried to angle his body away from her, she sucked in her breath. 'Oh, crap,' she said on an exhale. 'Did Zorro do this to you?'

'No,' he said dryly, struggling for normality. 'It was some other cat I put next to my stomach.'

'I'm sorry,' she said, and then she took the salve from him and began to smear it gently on his scratches. He felt his torso tremble—saw it, too, though he tried to ignore it—and hoped Ava wouldn't notice.

'I'm sorry,' she said again. 'Is it painful? It's a lot more enthusiastic than I'd expect from Zorro.'

'It's fine.' He gritted his teeth as her hand moved lower, down to the scratches near the waistband of his pants.

'Clearly it isn't.'

Her touch was still light, still gentle, but when she moved lower still he grabbed her wrist.

'It's fine, Ava.'

The words were said in a harsher voice than he'd intended, and her eyes widened. But that was better than having her move any lower and having his body respond in an unpredictable way—or a very predictable way. He was only just clinging to his control as it was.

'I'm—I'm sorry.'

'Don't be.'

He was still holding on to her hand, but he softened his voice. And then she looked at him and his world tilted.

Uh-oh.

What the hell was she *doing*?

She'd acted without thinking. Or she *had* been thinking, but not about how it would feel to be touching Noah's bare torso. No, she'd been thinking about how her cat had hurt him. How her cat had hurt him because of *her*. Because Noah had gone back to save Zorro so she wouldn't have to.

But she wasn't thinking about that now either.

In fact, she couldn't be sure that she was thinking at all. Because now she was caught in Noah's gaze when she was pretty sure she shouldn't be. He was so close she could see the grey flecks in his blue eyes. She could see the emotions there, too.

The caution. The interest. The *desire*.

It had her remembering that he still had her wrist in his hand. And that realisation sent a heady heat slithering from the contact, up and around her arm, settling much too close to her chest. To her heart.

Her other hand was still braced on the lower half of his body. Much too close to his—

'Um…' she said, pulling her hands from his body and stepping back. 'It's probably okay now.'

'Yeah,' he replied in a hoarse voice. He cleared his throat. 'It was fine before you came in.'

'Of course.'

There was an awkward beat of silence, but Ava took solace in the fact that it came from both of them. She hadn't been the only one acting stupidly. She hadn't been the only one affected.

But thinking about it like that didn't comfort her as much as she'd hoped.

'Could you pass me my top?' Noah asked after a few moments.

'Yeah, sure.' She paused. 'Where is it?'

'Behind you.'

When she turned back to hand it to him there was a slight smile on his face.

'What's so funny?'

'Nothing,' he said, pulling on his top.

Disappointment sailed through her as she said goodbye to his abs.

'I was just thinking it's going to be an interesting wedding.'

'That's one way to put it.'

'You don't think so?'

'I think that I need to get through it in any way that I can. Which,' she said, considering, 'might involve alcohol.'

'Ah. You're old enough to drink now, aren't you?'

She cocked an eyebrow. 'You say that as if *you* weren't the one who handed me my first beer.'

His smile widened. 'See—interesting.'

'You and I have *very* different definitions of that,' she replied, and walked back around the counter. Her breath came out a little more easily now that there was space between them.

'Probably. But I think it might have the same results.'

Which was precisely what she was worried about. Because after the short, but very eye-opening interaction they'd just had, she was beginning to think her crush was no longer a secret.

Or perhaps she was more concerned that this unexpected flare-up of her crush was no longer a secret. Because if she'd managed to keep it secret after she'd asked him to kiss her for the *first* time, she certainly hadn't after she'd thrown herself into their second kiss.

But in the seven years since they'd last seen one another—years during which she hadn't even *heard* from him—she had managed to hide her feelings. And if what had just happened between them meant that Noah shared those feelings—

Noah? Sharing her feelings?

She nearly laughed aloud at the ludicrousness of it. She'd always known the reason he'd kissed her the first time had been out of pity.

And the second kiss had just happened because he'd been heartbroken and hadn't known *what* he was feeling.

Anything they'd shared was in her imagination. Back then *and* now. No one wanted Ava. No one wanted someone who spoke before she thought. Who was prickly for most of the time and defensive for the rest.

Just because Milo said it doesn't make it true.

But it does, she corrected the voice in her head.

Milo hadn't wanted to marry her after being with her for five years. He was the best person to know the truth. And if he hadn't wanted her Noah sure as hell wouldn't either.

The sooner she realised that, the better.

He was back from the deli in less than fifteen minutes. Ava had graciously allowed him to leave without commenting on the fact that he was buying their food. But maybe it wasn't grace. Maybe she just needed space to deal with what had happened between them, just as he had.

It was a natural reaction to being around a beautiful woman, he'd told himself on the way to the deli. He hadn't dated in so long he couldn't remember. His body had just been reminding him that he had needs; his mind just responding as any person who had needs would.

But when he returned and saw Ava sitting on his balcony, staring out over the mountains visible to most residents of Somerset West, he faltered. Had she looked this forlorn before? This defenceless?

Now she seemed nothing like the spitfire who had tried to save her cat from a blaze and everything like that little girl he'd once saved from being bullied. And when his heart turned in his chest and his arms ached to pull her into his arms, Noah worried that his reaction to her earlier hadn't just been natural. That it had been…*more.*

It didn't help that when her eyes met his— brown and steady—he instinctively knew she *wasn't* that little girl who'd needed saving. Her gaze wasn't as innocent, as trusting, as that little girl's had been. It was weary, cautious—as if she were ready to defend herself at any moment.

'This place is just as beautiful on the outside as it is on the inside,' she said into the silence.

Grateful for the distraction—his thoughts

bothered him more than he'd thought they should—he nodded. 'This particular view sealed the deal for me.'

'I can imagine.' She pushed out from the table she'd been sitting at. 'I'd love to enjoy it some more, but I'm hungry. Like, *really* hungry. What do you have in there?'

He swung the deli bags out of her reach when she tried to peek inside them, and thought about how similar this was to how they'd been before he'd left. How similar it was to how *she'd* been before. And how it didn't make him feel like he needed to protect her.

'You'll find out when I serve it.'

'Spoilsport.' She followed him to the kitchen. 'Can I help?'

'No.'

'Excuse me?'

He smiled at the disbelief in her voice, and then took his time removing the takeaway dishes from the plastic bag and placing them on the kitchen counter.

When he saw her hovering, he said, 'Have a seat.'

'You're really refusing my help?'

'Yes.' He opened his fridge, showing her different drinks one by one until she eventually nodded at the fruit juice he took out. 'I didn't ask you here so you could help me cook, Ava.'

'I think you're using the word *cook* wrong,' she commented dryly, and then took the glass he offered her and went to the couch.

He could almost see her body sag into its softness. He was glad he'd refused her help.

'You know, the last time I was at your house—and this was when you still lived with your father—you didn't know what "cook" meant then either. I think you gave me and Jaden leftovers from the night before.'

'How do you know I didn't cook the night before?'

'Because it was delicious.' She smiled brightly at the look he gave her. 'And because your father's made me a few more of those pasta dishes since you left and it was definitely not *your* cooking.'

His hands paused. 'You've seen my father since I've been away?'

He saw her cheeks pinken. 'Yeah... I mean, occasionally...' She cleared her throat. 'I've been helping him with some stuff. We're... friends.'

The pink turned into a deep red, and if Noah hadn't been so perplexed by the whole thing—

if his heart hadn't been racing in his chest—
he'd have found it charming.

'So, just to check that I've heard you cor-
rectly,' he said slowly, when his brain refused
to process what she'd told him, 'you say you're
friends with my father?'

'Don't make it sound so outlandish, Noah,'
she said with a roll of her eyes. Her embarrassment seemed to have worn off. 'Your father is incredibly interesting. And he's young
for his age. I can barely tell he's in his sixties.'
She sipped her juice. 'And, while we're at it, I
might as well tell you that by "occasionally" I
actually mean at least every two weeks. More
often if my schedule—and his—can manage
it.' She lifted her shoulders at the look on his
face. 'We enjoy each other's company, Noah.
There's nothing wrong with that.'

All the blood seemed to drain from his body.

'Ava,' he said, his voice strangled. 'Are you
trying... Are you trying to tell me that you're
in a relationship with my father?'

CHAPTER FIVE

AVA STARED AT him for what felt like for ever. And then she choked back a laugh and used the opportunity.

'I'm sorry, Noah,' she said solemnly. 'We didn't want you to find out this way.'

His jaw dropped, and it took every bit of her self-control not to show her enjoyment.

'But…but…how? *Why?*'

'I don't think I have to explain *how*,' she said matter-of-factly. Man, she was really getting to use her acting skills today. 'I mean, I know for a fact that *you* know how to kiss. And, sure, there's some other stuff which I'd be happy to—'

'Ava.'

His voice had taken on a quality Ava had never heard before.

'Please do *not* allude to your sex life with my father.'

She bit her lip so hard she was afraid she'd draw blood. 'We're all adults, Noah.'

'No, we're not. You're still a *kid*.'

He was angry now, and Ava tried not to let him thinking of her as a kid bother her.

'You've been gone for a long time, Noah. I'm not a kid any more.'

'My father,' he repeated in a daze. 'My *father*.'

'Yes.' She paused. 'You asked me why earlier. I've already told you some of it. He's interesting. And kind. And he's got such a sweet heart. And an impressive—'

'Do *not* finish that sentence.'

'Why not?' she asked innocently. 'I was only going to say he has an impressive…' she dragged out the pause for as long as she could '…personality.'

He stared at her. 'You've got to be kidding me.'

She contemplated whether she should just say yes, she *was* kidding him. But there was one more thing she wanted to say first…

'You know, Noah, you not being at home has been really hard on your father. And, as your possible stepmother, I wanted—'

'Ava!' he barked, his expression stricken.

And, because she'd done what she wanted to, she grinned at him. 'You are *such* a sucker, Giles.'

There was a long silence before his features relaxed. Only slightly though, she noted.

'You were joking.'

'I was.'

Another stretch of silence. 'What made you think that joke would be *funny*?'

She laughed. 'The entire time I kept it going?'

She laughed harder when he threw the empty juice bottle at her, and she caught it triumphantly.

'You're going to have to try better than that.'

'Yeah, well, let me first get over the heart attack I've just had.'

She chuckled to herself as he prepared their food, still muttering, but when he brought over her plate—chicken, a portion of lasagne, potato salad, coleslaw—she gaped.

'Who do you think you're feeding? The South African army?'

'You said you were hungry.'

'Yeah, but I meant for a normal human-sized person.' She dug into the meal anyway, almost hearing the food echo as it dropped into her empty stomach. 'Thank you,' she said gratefully.

'Yeah, no problem.'

A companionable silence fell over them as they ate, and for the first time Ava realised how tired—and hungry—Noah must be. She saw the dark tint under his eyes, the slight creases around them.

'You should go to bed,' she said softly. 'You look exhausted.'

'Thanks.'

He gave her a small smile that had her heart flipping over.

'You don't look too great yourself.'

'Ah, I've missed this insult-for-insult thing we've always had.'

'Hmm…' he said, non-committal, and took another bite of lasagne, watching her all the time.

She refused to shift in her seat. Refused to look away. Even though she desperately wanted to do both. Tension ticked up.

'You didn't say it before,' he said after he'd swallowed.

'What?'

'That you missed me.'

'What do you mean?' Now she *did* shift. 'It's not just something you say when you see someone after a long time.'

'It's *exactly* the kind of thing you say when you see someone after a long time.'

'Yes, well…'

She left it at that, unsure of what else to say.

The conversation was wading into dangerous waters and she, for one, had no interest in swimming. She just wanted to stand safely in the sand and frolic on the beach. She just wanted to feel the sun on her skin and *maybe* put her toes in the water.

But swimming held no appeal to her.

'Is it because—'

'Noah,' she interrupted with a half-smile. 'We've been through enough today. I think we should probably leave this conversation for another time.'

He studied her, and again she refused to let him see how uncomfortable it made her.

'Sure,' he said, and then he nodded at her plate. 'Are you done with that?'

Noah woke to a house that was significantly less festive than the one he'd gone to sleep in. But, he thought, as he took in the tinsel that now hung only over his fireplace—along with the stockings and the lights—and the significantly fewer Christmas-related items around the house, it was perfect.

He didn't know what to say when he found Ava by his Christmas tree. She had tinsel over each shoulder, draped around her neck, too, and was taking some of the ornaments off the ridiculously overdone tree.

Just as he had the night before, he watched her. She was muttering to herself, occasionally bopping her head as if she were listening to music only she could hear. It was so homely it was almost enticing, and he had to step back, out of her range of view, to deal with how that made him feel.

He wasn't interested in *homely*. He'd thought he'd once *had* homely—until he'd been old enough to realise the man he'd seen in his parents' bedroom when he was younger hadn't been his mother's *friend*. It hadn't been his father either. But by the time he'd been old enough to realise that his mother had passed away and his anger had seemed pointless.

Not that that had stopped the anger from finding a home, he thought, as he remembered the women who had come in and out of his life—of his father's life—after his mother's death. The women who'd never stayed long but had always left his father with that sad look on his face.

The same look his father had had when he'd confirmed that Noah's mother *had* cheated on him the one time they'd spoken about it.

If that hadn't put Noah off *homely*, his own attempt at it had taught him a lesson. A lesson his heart and his mind still hadn't forgiven him for.

So what was wrong with him now? Why did he feel drawn to the image Ava was creating by that Christmas tree?

He'd been back all of two weeks. He'd been reunited with her all of twenty-four hours. *Barely* that. Maybe that was why he felt as if something were wrong. Because it *was*. There was no possible way he could want something he'd never wanted before after only two weeks. There was no possible way he could want it with a woman he'd only been back in touch with for barely twenty-four hours after seven years.

What about the eighteen years before that? And what about that kiss?

His spine stiffened. Ava had told him last night that she didn't want to talk about the kiss. Not explicitly, but he'd got the picture. And he couldn't blame her. The only reason he'd even brought it up was because he'd thought *she'd* want to talk about it.

But, no. It seemed they were going to pretend it hadn't happened.

He took a moment to compose himself—it took longer than he would have liked—and then strolled into the living room.

'Mrs Claus?' He forced a cheer he didn't feel into his voice. 'Is that you?'

'Why, yes, little elf, it is.'

She turned to him, eyes twinkling, and he was immediately drawn back into the memory he'd just tried to suppress…

'Jaden is taking for *ever.*'

'His speciality,' Noah replied. 'He and Monica are probably making out somewhere.'

Ava's face twisted in disgust. 'Why would you put that image in my head? I'm perfectly happy thinking about my brother as a monk.'

Noah snorted. 'Jaden is *not* a monk.'

'Stop it.'

'You're an adult now, Ava,' he said with a smirk. 'At least, almost.'

'I'm *eighteen.*'

'Like I said—*almost* an adult.'

She narrowed her eyes at him. 'Just because I don't want to hear about my brother's sex habits doesn't mean I'm not an adult.'

'You're *eighteen.*'

She rolled her eyes. 'Yeah, and you were *such* a kid when you were eighteen.'

He had been, he thought. He'd made all kinds of stupid decisions between the age of eighteen and now. Most notably falling hard and fast for a woman who had no intention of committing to him. Worse yet, a woman who had shown him he was at risk of following in his father's footsteps.

'We should probably head to the pools without him,' Noah said after a few more minutes. 'We don't want to get there and have them turn us away.'

Ava nodded and walked ahead of him along the path to the pools. It was going to be thirty-eight degrees Celsius that day, and they'd decided—Noah, Jaden, Monica and Ava—to survive the heat by going to the natural rock pools near Noah's house.

They weren't private pools, but because they were situated in an ecologically sensitive area that the government only allowed twelve people access to per day. There were already four of them, so they'd got up extra early to take the short hike to the rock pools.

Or at least that had been the plan before Jaden hadn't shown up.

'You'd have thought he'd have told you he'd be late,' Noah commented.

'He doesn't do things just because we think

he should,' Ava said with a sigh. 'He told me last night that he'd meet us at the starting point. His excuse then was that he needed to fetch Monica.'

'Why didn't you go with him?'

'Because he was meant to be spending the night at *your* house.' She gave him a look. 'Even though my brother is two years older than me, he still isn't an adult.'

'That lie was more for your parents,' Noah said, automatically defending his friend, even though Jaden was the reason Ava had taken that jibe at him.

'Yeah, well, he could have at least had the decency to pitch up on time.'

They didn't speak for the rest of the trip. In fact the only communication they had with one another was when Ava missed a step on an incline and called out, and he pushed forward to help steady her.

His hands rested on her hips, just above her butt, and long after he'd let go his fingers could still feel the softness—the plumpness—of her there. It made him *want* her—which was ridiculous. She was Jaden's *sister*. And he'd just dodged a massive bullet with Tiff. The last thing on his mind was wanting anyone—let alone the girl he'd once seen smell her armpits to test whether she needed to start wearing deodorant.

It was ridiculous, he thought again. Except his eyes dipped to the rounded curve of her butt in her cotton shorts. To her thighs, which were thick and strong and made him think things he shouldn't be thinking about his best friend's little sister.

It put him in a mood, which kept him silent until they reached the entrance of the pools and were told they were the first there.

'Yes!'

They high-fived each other, and then Ava turned to the guard. 'Is it okay for us to keep places for my brother and his girlfriend? They're slower than us, so we went ahead to could get spots for all of us.'

She smiled widely at the man, and Noah watched as he blinked and then nodded. Sympathy pooled in his stomach. He didn't think *he'd* be able to resist that smile either. It was the kind that could make anyone feel blinded. Combined with Ava's naturally husky voice, its effect was potent.

But he *had* resisted that smile, he told himself. And he still did. All the time. In fact he barely noticed that it made her eyes crinkle. Or that it softened her features, making her look like some kind of mythical creature.

Man, what had Tiff *done* to him?

'Noah?'

He blinked, his gaze zooming in on her.

'You didn't hear a word I said, did you?'

'Er...yeah, of course I did.'

'Liar.'

His lips curved. 'You want to know whether this is a good spot to sit in.'

She narrowed her eyes. 'That's a logical deduction. It's not because you were listening to me.' She tossed her head back. 'So, is it?'

His smile widened. 'It's perfect.'

They set up the blankets and umbrellas they'd brought, but by the time they were done Jaden and Monica still hadn't arrived. Neither had anyone else.

'Screw this,' Ava said after a moment. 'I'm hot, I've walked further than I generally do most days, and I deserve a swim.'

She was pulling off her top and wriggling off her shorts before he could say anything to stop her. And by the time he could he found that his voice was gone. Stolen by how beautiful her body was.

She's off-limits...she's off-limits...she's off-limits.

He repeated the words inside his head, over and over again, hoping it would drown out the other voice in his head pointing out how beautiful the brown skin of her body was against the white of her bikini. How the rounding of her breasts, her hips, was the stuff of fantasies. How they would be the stuff of *his* fantasies in the future.

She's off-limits...she's off-limits...she's-off limits.

She gave him a smile he didn't understand, and then she threw her clothes at him. The pile landed against his chest, his hands barely lifting in time to keep everything from falling to the ground. And then she turned and his heart hammered, his body tightening as he got a better view of the butt he'd been admiring earlier.

With one sly look over her shoulder, Ava ran and dived into the water.

It took all the time she was under the water for him to realise that she'd been trying to seduce him. But his mind rejected that explanation even as it pointed out all the ways her actions had been an attempt at seduction.

Before he knew it he was pulling off his T-shirt and following her into the water. When he emerged, he found himself a short distance from her.

'Cooler now?' he asked, surprised at how steady his voice was.

'Never been cooler.'

Her eyes were twinkling, her expression teasing, but there was a seriousness there, too, somehow, and he wondered if that could be more seduction.

'This isn't in my head, is it?' she asked him softly.

'I don't know what you're talking about.'

She gave him a small smile. 'So maybe we should keep it like that, then. We'll pretend like you aren't looking at me the way you are now. That I didn't say anything about it—about us—at all.' She paused. 'We can pretend it didn't happen—just like after the first time we kissed.'

'You asked me—'

'You could have said no,' she interrupted him. 'In fact, you *should* have said no. I'm your best friend's sister. You had no business kissing me.'

'I know.' Somehow he found himself even closer to her.

'Why would you want to be my first kiss, Noah?'

'You asked me to be.'

'And now I'll always have the story of how my brother's best friend kissed me for the first time.'

'You were sixteen. Too old not to have been kissed.'

She laughed—low, husky—and it vibrated through his body. 'Is there a timeline for that I don't know about?'

'Yes.'

'Like the rules about who your first kiss should be with?'

'Honestly, I don't care.' And in that moment Noah thought he'd lost his mind. 'I don't care about the rules and the ages.'

'Because you *wanted* to kiss me.'

'Yes.'

'Just like you do now.'

He didn't answer her. Only slid a hand around her waist and pulled her against him as their lips met.

CHAPTER SIX

'WHAT?' AVA ASKED, when the silence extended much too long for her liking. When the expression on Noah's face went from easy to tight and the emotion rippling across his features made her stomach tremble.

'Nothing.' His voice was hoarse.

'Are you okay?' She dropped the ornament she held in her hands to the couch and moved forward. 'Should I take you to the doctor? Back to the hospital?'

'No.' His voice was stronger now. 'No,' he said again. 'I'm fine. I just got a little... distracted.'

The air moved more easily into her lungs. 'By what? I thought you were about to have a heart attack.'

'Sorry,' he said. Still, she heard the strain. 'This looks great, by the way. You didn't have to do it.'

'I know,' she said, and picked up the ornament she'd dropped, putting it with the others.

'But it was the least I could do after you took such great care of me and Zorro yesterday.'

He studied her, and as the seconds ticked by Ava tried not to wriggle under his gaze.

'You couldn't sleep, huh?'

She laughed, but the words jolted her. How had he known? 'I slept fine.'

He arched a brow.

She hissed out a breath. 'Fine. I slept okay for the first bit, and then I woke up and my mind started thinking about everything that happened and everything that's going to happen and I couldn't go back to sleep.' She forced a smile. 'At least it's the weekend.'

'Hell of a time to have to think about your house burning down.'

She shrugged, though sadness wove through her. 'I haven't had the heart to check.'

'I'll call the station.'

Ava continued removing the ornaments from the Christmas tree while he went outside to make the call. As she did so, she wondered why she hadn't told him that her house had been at the bottom of the list of things she was worried about. At the top of the list was whether Noah was okay and whether Zorro was.

Because early that morning she'd realised

again how much danger she'd put him in by having him go back for Zorro. The smoke could have had a worse effect than she'd imagined. Because, of course, as that thought had occurred to her she'd done an internet search on smoke inhalation and found out the most horrific things. Things even that TV show hadn't prepared her for.

Which had got her thinking about Zorro. And how, though she hated it that she'd put Noah in danger, she couldn't bring herself to regret it. She'd thought about all the times she'd cried and Zorro had curled up near her. Not anywhere close to her body—he was still a cat—but close enough that she'd understood he was offering her as much comfort as a cat could.

She'd thought about how he'd helped her stave off loneliness when it had threatened to overwhelm her. When thoughts of how much she needed to change had kept her up at night. When the hopelessness that she wouldn't be able to change had done the same. As had the fear that no one would ever love her. Zorro had kept her calm through it all.

And then, of course, she'd thought about the wedding. And the fact that she was being forced to participate in it when it was the last thing—the *very* last thing—in the entire world she wanted to do.

She was fully aware of the resentment that had come along with that thought. Fully aware that it had spilled over too many times during the planning of Leela's bachelorette party, which—thankfully—was now behind her. She had worried that during these last two weeks her resentment would spill over in ways she wouldn't know how to clean up.

'Well, the fire is still ongoing,' Noah said as he walked back into the room. 'But the wind's shifted, which means the direction of the fire has changed.'

'Away from the estate?'

'Yes,' he said, and started helping her remove more decorations from the tree. 'They're waiting for the smoke to subside and then they'll check everything out. It might still be a while before you can move back in, though.'

'Oh. *Oh...*' she said again, on an exhale. 'That makes me feel better than I thought it would.'

He frowned. 'I thought you were worried about your house?'

'I was. I *am.*' She stood on her tiptoes to get to the higher parts of the tree. 'But there are other things, too.'

'Like what?'

'Oh, you know...' She didn't elaborate, and though the silence that fell between them felt expectant—as if it wanted Ava to elaborate too—they both let it extend.

'I know you were pulling my leg about you and my father yesterday,' Noah said after a while.

His tone was casual, but Ava knew he was fighting to achieve it.

'But before that conversation went so terribly wrong, I did get the impression you were friends with him.'

'I am.'

With most of the decorations off, she reached up for the angel at the top of the tree. It was higher than she could reach, but she managed to touch the bottom of it. Thinking she could tip it over, she jumped and tried again. Except that did nothing except make the branches of the tree rustle.

'Here.'

It was the only warning she got before Noah's hands were on her hips, lifting her.

Her breath whooshed from her lungs and heat spread through her body. It felt intimate, this completely innocent gesture of his, and it charged the air around her. Around *them*, she thought, when she glanced down and saw the expression on his face.

She reached up for the angel quickly, thinking that as soon as she got it down they'd go back to being easy around one another. Except when he put her down and she turned to put the angel with the other decorations she was faced with his chest. And though it was covered by his T-shirt, she could still see the muscles of it.

Which wasn't a surprise, since a picture of him without his top on had been seared into her brain the day before. No, she thought immediately. A *long* time ago. Specifically, the day he'd followed her into that water and she'd had the opportunity to run her hands over every glorious inch of it...

Her fingers itched to do it again. His body was different now. Bigger. Stronger. And she wanted new memories that could replace the ones she visited on particularly hard days. Which also made her think that she'd lied when she'd told herself that her relationship with Milo had stopped her from thinking about Noah.

'Excuse me,' she said softly as the thought shook her.

She put the angel on the couch and took another step back, suddenly thankful Noah hadn't closed the door after he'd made his call and a slight breeze was blowing through the house.

'So,' she said very deliberately, 'I know putting a Christmas tree up is a sacred thing, but—'

'It isn't.'

'What?'

'Sacred.'

She frowned. 'Of course it is. It's a pivotal part of mentally preparing for Christmas.'

'Okay,' he agreed. 'But it's not sacred.'

'Noah,' she said with forced patience. 'How many times have you helped us put up our tree? You know it's sacred. We do it and we have dessert and fruit after, along with whatever cold drink we desire.' She frowned. 'You *know* this.'

'I know that's how *you* celebrate it, Avalanche.'

He lowered himself to the couch, and something about the movement made her think he hadn't slept well either.

'But my dad usually did our tree on his own. I'd get home and it was already done.'

'So you came to celebrate with us?'

'No, I just visited.' She gave him a look and

he smiled. 'So I came to celebrate it with you. So what?'

She thought about it for all of two seconds. 'Get dressed.'

'What?'

'Get dressed. We're going to the shop. First, to buy me something a bit more presentable for being out in public,' she said, frowning down at his clothes which she still wore. 'And as soon as we've done that we're going to buy something nice for breakfast. Chocolate croissants, eclairs…maybe a fruit platter so we don't feel entirely guilty about our life choices. And then, dear Noah, we're going to decorate your tree.'

'This wasn't such a bad idea after all,' Noah said an hour later, when they were back from the shops and were taking a pre-tree-decorating break on the balcony.

Ava shot him a look. 'Oh, please. You complained from the moment I suggested it. And now that we have this delicious spread—' she gestured to the breakfast they'd bought, consisting mostly, if not completely, of the kind of food she'd suggested earlier '—you're changing your mind.'

'I'm an adult,' he said mildly. 'I can change my mind as and when I see fit.'

She grunted and popped a piece of croissant into her mouth. He grinned at the inelegance of it. He might not be prepared to think about the more uncomfortable moments or memories being around Ava brought, but he still enjoyed spending time with her.

'Okay, so,' she said after a moment, 'it might seem like I'm dodging your question about your father, but I'm not.'

'Hence you bringing it up now?'

'Exactly.' She gave him a winning smile. 'A couple of years ago Jaden asked me to drop off something you'd sent for your father after the last time the two of you had seen one another.'

'It was the magazine my pictures were in.'

'Yeah. A small magazine with, like, a ten-person readership.'

It had been an international magazine with thousands of readers. He smiled.

'Anyway, something came up, but Jaden had already promised your dad he'd bring it over. So I took it, and Kirk invited me in for a drink—completely platonically,' she added dryly, 'and we started talking. And became friends.'

Noah sat back, his coffee in his hand. 'Sounds simple.'

'Don't make it sound like there was some *thing* that had to happen for us to be friends.' She tilted her head. 'Or wait—maybe there was. He'd just finalised his divorce—'

'His fourth.'

'And he wanted some company,' she finished, as if he hadn't interrupted her.

'What do *you* get out of it?'

She sighed. 'I don't know. Like I told you yesterday, he's a lovely man. And he's wise.'

'Not wise enough to stay away from marriage.' Anger and resentment rippled through him.

'Noah,' she said in a low tone.

It sounded like disappointment. He wasn't sure why that stung. Or why it felt worse than anger.

'Besides, I guess that other than that it was a way for me to get away from wedding planning. It takes up your entire life and makes you feel worse than you can imagine.' She rolled her eyes. 'And it's supposed to be the best day of your life.'

'What are you talking about? Leela and Jaden weren't even engaged two years ago.'

'Yeah, I know.' She stared at him. 'You don't remember, do you?'

He frowned. 'Don't remember what?'

'Or maybe you don't even know,' she said softly, almost to herself.

And then she laughed, but the sound of it was strangled and it had his stomach turning.

'I'm sorry, I hadn't realised.' Her eyes met his, and there was pain and a sick kind of amusement in them. 'I'm talking about *my* wedding, Noah.'

CHAPTER SEVEN

'*YOUR* WEDDING?' HE REPEATED.

'Yes,' she said calmly, but she broke off flakes of crust from her croissant, undermining the tone. 'I was supposed to be married now.'

The thought of it had his mind spinning. A sick feeling stumbled through his stomach. An ache echoed through his chest.

'Clearly I'm missing something here. Why don't you start at the beginning?'

'There's not much to tell,' she said, in a way that made him think there was. 'I started dating a guy about a year after you left.'

A light blush spread over her cheeks, though he wasn't sure why.

'We were together for four years before he proposed. And we were engaged for a year before he left me at the altar.'

'He—' If he'd thought his mind had been spinning earlier, it had nothing on what was happening inside of his head now. 'A guy you were in a serious relationship with for five years left you at the altar? What the—'

'I appreciate the sentiment,' she interjected, with a smile that was half amused, half sad. 'I shared it. Still do some days.'

She went quiet for a moment, and when her eyes met his there was pain there that illogically he wanted to fix.

'But I'm over it.'

She'd never been a good liar. 'I'm sorry, Avalanche.'

'Thank you.'

A beat of silence passed. He wanted to say something about how relationships weren't worth the pain. Or point out that this was the exact reason why he didn't want to get involved with anyone. But it didn't seem like the right thing to say, especially when part of it was a lie.

He didn't want to get involved with anyone because he was terrified that history would repeat itself. And Noah had no intention of living his life in the same way his father lived his.

'You were going to get married and you didn't invite me?' he said, deciding on a more innocuous route.

But as soon as he'd said it, and emotion tightened in his chest, he realised it wasn't so innocuous after all.

'I was going to get married and I *did* invite you. I just never got a response to my email. Just like with all the others I sent.'

He opened his mouth to ask what email, but froze as dread filled him. The night after they'd kissed—after he'd felt things he never should have for his best friend's younger sister…after he'd been *caught*—he'd blocked Ava's email address.

Pre-emptively, he'd thought back then, because he hadn't wanted her to ask him why he was leaving without saying goodbye. Why, after they'd kissed, he'd decided to take advantage of an opportunity he'd been avoiding deciding on for a month. He hadn't wanted her to ask him whether that decision had anything to do with her. In fact, he'd wanted her to think it had *nothing* to do with her and everything to do with how things had ended with Tiff.

A stupid hope, he knew.

Just like the stupid decision he'd made when he hadn't known any better. Because of it he'd missed out on seven years of Ava's life. He hadn't heard from her and hadn't wanted to contact her. Hadn't thought he'd had the right to in case she was avoiding him purposely.

'Ava, I'm so—'

'Nope. *No*,' she said, in a tone that was a little too bright, with a smile that was a little too bright. 'Don't apologise. You were travelling around the world. Photographing new and exciting things. You don't have to apologise for not replying to my emails.'

'I do.' He braced his wrists on the table. 'I blocked your email address.' Shame rose in his throat as he took in the expression on her face. 'After the...er...the kiss—' *real mature, Noah* '—I blocked it.'

'You *blocked* my email address?' she repeated. 'After you kissed me, you blocked my emails?'

Her voice had gone thin, and it felt like a warning. But he had to face the fact that he'd made a mistake. It was the only way he could redeem himself.

'It was a stupid thing to do. I was an immature kid, and—'

'After you kissed me.' She slammed a hand on the table. '*You* kissed *me*, Noah.'

'I know.'

And now his shame had nothing to do with

how she was responding and everything to do with how he'd crossed a boundary with her—with Jaden—that he'd never be able to erase.

'I'm sorry.'

She tossed her head back and looked up. If he didn't know any better he'd wonder if she was crying. But Ava didn't cry. He hadn't seen her cry since that girl had bullied her. It had been a watershed moment for her, he thought. The girl had *wanted* to make her cry; Ava had refused to give her what she wanted. And since then Ava had refused to cry in front of people in general.

He knew because he'd asked her about it. Long before the day they'd kissed. Which was why he knew that the betrayal and hurt on her face after Jaden had caught them—and Noah had then ignored her—would be the worst she'd let him see. He'd respected her for it, even as disgust had pooled inside him.

Exactly like now.

But, unlike then, when her eyes met his now they were clear of emotion. 'It's okay. We were both kids. It was a mistake.'

Was it?

He didn't ask. It wouldn't have been fair.

'Besides,' she continued, 'I got the information I needed from Jaden. That you were safe.'

She answered his silent question. 'And when I started hanging out with your father I got it from him.' She paused. 'Life goes on.'

He didn't reply to that. The morning had been an overload of information that he wasn't ready to dwell on. But even as he thought that questions sprang to his mind.

She'd been engaged? She'd invited him to the wedding? Why hadn't Jaden told him? Why hadn't his father? She was friends with his father? Why did he feel betrayed? Confused? Raw?

The thoughts were unwelcome, as were the emotions. Acknowledging either was bound to lead him down a path he had no intention of travelling. The path of examining his past. Of facing his mistakes. Doing it with Ava about blocking her emails was enough for that day.

Except the universe seemed to have another idea.

'Tiff's going to be there, you know. At the wedding.'

Immediately after she'd said it she regretted it. Partly because she knew Jaden had wanted to tell Noah that the woman who'd broken his heart would be part of the wedding. Mostly be-

cause the stunned, strained expression on Noah's face wreaked havoc on her heart.

*You're hurt and now you're lashing out, hurt-
ing other people in the process.*

She squeezed her eyes shut—trying to ignore the voice that confirmed she was a terrible person—and focused on the upside. She'd
done the right thing. Jaden should have told
Noah about Tiff coming ages ago. He should
have given Noah the opportunity to opt out of
being his best man as soon as he'd known Tiff
was going to be a bridesmaid.

'I'm sorry, did you just say Tiff is going to
be at this wedding?'

'*In* the wedding. She's the maid of honour.'

He swore and shook his head. 'How the hell
did *that* happen?'

'Because the world is cruel and does things
like this all the time.'

'Your ex isn't going to be there, too, is he?'

She laughed at the incredulity of his tone, and
relief rippled through her when it broke some
of the tension.

'No, thankfully not. But Jaden *is* getting married almost to the day when my wedding was
supposed to happen last year, so I still think
the world is cruel.'

'He's—' Noah broke off with a shake of his

head. 'What the hell happened? It sounds like Jaden thought about what would hurt the people he loved the most, and then decided to do just that.'

'It's not entirely his fault,' she said in his defence, though she'd been blaming him for a while. 'He was outnumbered. Leela wanted to get married close to Christmas, and the venue only had this date available. Tiff is also one of Leela's friends,' she added. 'I hate to break it to you, but she's responsible for introducing Jaden and Leela.'

'How?'

'Jaden bumped into Tiff at a restaurant and was forced to greet her. She was with Leela, and there was enough of a spark between the two of them that they exchanged numbers. So...' She considered. 'Not entirely his fault.'

'He still should have told me.'

'Absolutely. Which I kept telling him. But he said he wanted to tell you in person.'

'A heads-up over the telephone—or even an email—would have been appreciated.'

'Maybe we should give him the benefit of the doubt.'

Noah made a low sound in his throat and, taking in the look on his face, Ava giggled.

'It's not funny.'

'Oh, absolutely not,' she said, and laughed some more. 'But I can't keep being mad about this, Noah. It's *exhausting. I'm* exhausted.' Her laugh turned into a hiccup of despair. 'See what I mean? I'm tired of this. And of feeling this way. So I'm going to laugh and try to get through this *stupid* wedding, where every member of my family is going to look at me with sympathy, or ask me why I haven't moved on yet, or how my year has been. *Urgh.*'

She tilted her head back and tried to gain some semblance of control over her emotions again.

'Tell them it's none of their business,' Noah said after a moment. 'And then ask them about the most inappropriate thing you've heard about them.'

'What?'

He was grinning when she looked at him. 'You know how we keep hearing things about our family members? Like my uncle has two kids no one talks about. *Two.* So, my suggestion is, if someone asks you about how you've been doing, or makes some reference to the wedding, you ask about the two kids no one's talking about.'

She stared at him, and then grinned. 'That is the most brilliant thing I've ever heard.'

CHAPTER EIGHT

'WELL, THEN,' HE SAID, on a roll now, 'prepare yourself for something even better.'

'Not possible.'

'Oh, but it is.' He waited a beat. 'I don't think I'm going to like this wedding any more than you're going to.'

She narrowed her eyes. 'Continue.'

'And since I don't have any family there to embarrass—except maybe my dad, and he's as open as they come about his mistakes—maybe you and I should make a little wager.'

'A wager?' Ava sat back and rested her legs on the chair in front of her. 'You intrigue me, Mr Giles. What are the terms of this wager?'

'If you're going to try and put your family members on the spot, you'll have to do it in front of me. I'll give you points for how well you do it.'

'And in return?'

'You entertain me.'

'Oh, no. No, no, no,' she said with a laugh. 'That's not a *wager*.'

'It is. I'll bet you that you can't get a thousand points.'

'How dare you? Of *course* I'll get to a thousand points.' She paused. 'We'll discuss the determination of points later. But first I have to point out that I'm not really getting anything out of this bet. And, no, entertaining you doesn't count.'

'Okay, fine,' he said with a grin. He was enjoying this process almost as much as he was enjoying seeing the light back in her eyes. He hadn't realised until it was gone how much he cherished it. 'What do you want?'

'Hmm…let me see. Money would be too easy for you.'

'I'm fine with money.'

'No,' she said, with a smile that made his body ache. '*I'd* like to be entertained, too.'

The thought gave him visions of the two of them in that rock pool again. He shook his head. He was still recovering from his first memory. And from the feel of her waist under his hands. And from the way she'd looked at him afterwards, when she'd turned and he'd been so tempted to kiss her. And then from the reminder that he had no business being tempted by her, especially after what she'd just told him she'd gone through.

'I propose this,' she said, interrupting his thoughts. *Thank heaven.* 'We both try to entertain each other. It can come in the form of me saying inappropriate things to my family, or you doing something silly like…singing a song during the reception. Just an idea,' she said with a grin when he opened his mouth to protest. 'Whoever reaches a thousand points first, wins.'

'I'm *so* proud of how much you've grown into this,' he said with mock pride. 'I accept your proposal. I do, however, want to know how the scoring is going to work.'

'We have to witness the other person doing things in order to give points.'

'Fair.' He paused. 'The points are given in tens. From ten to one hundred.'

'One hundred is the maximum?'

'Unless there's a spectacular opportunity to take it all.'

'Take it all?' she repeated. 'As in win?'

'Yes.' A ripple of excitement went through him. 'Like doing a song during the reception.'

'I like it.' She bit her lip. 'Okay, but before we continue, this *can't* ruin Jaden and Leela's wedding. So, sadly, no singing. Unless, of course, we've received permission.'

'I completely agree.'

'So how are we going to score points?'

'Ah, that's harder.' Leaning in, he said, 'How about dealer decides? It'll be open for discussion, of course, but we each decide how much we want to give the other.'

'Fine, but there should be ranges. Ten to fifty points if we do something to defend ourselves. The two secret children thing, for example.'

He nodded.

'Sixty to a hundred points if we do something to defend the other person.' The side of her mouth curved. 'So, if Tiff says something about how you look, for instance, I'll just mention how much *she's* changed.'

'Into a decrepit old woman?'

She let out a sparkling laugh. 'Fifty points to you. But, no, just how much better she looks as a brunette than a redhead.'

'Sixty points. Seventy if the delivery was good.'

'Perfect,' she said, and leaned forward, stretching out her hand. 'Do we have a deal?'

'We do.' He started forward, but paused. 'Wait—when is the start, and when is the finish?'

Just as she opened her mouth her phone rang from where it was charging in the kitchen. She ran inside the house and a few minutes later reappeared.

'That was Jaden.' She blew out a breath. 'After I reassured him—again—that I'm fine, he wanted to know if I could meet him at the Stellenbosch Christmas Market. Apparently their visit to the venue has encouraged them to spend more time with the wedding party. They want us there.' She rolled her eyes. 'I expect you're going to get a phone call, too.'

Seconds later her prediction proved true. The conversation was quick, and when Noah hung up Ava said, 'I guess we're starting today.'

'And the winner will be declared at the end of the wedding. Deal?'

'Deal.'

They shook hands.

Ava knew how significant her deal—wager, bet—with Noah was. By agreeing to it she was making sure she wouldn't be alone during the wedding, or during the run-up to it. And, while it had started out as a way to distract them both from the wedding, having an ally would do more than just distract Ava.

It would help with the loneliness she'd felt during this process, since she was the only one who wasn't looking forward to the event. It would help her keep up the pretence that she was fine. Unhappy about the wedding, but completely fine within herself.

Which was a lie, but no one had to know that. Hell, at the best of times she managed to ignore it herself.

At the worst of times she tried to figure out how she could turn herself into someone more palatable. And then she'd wonder if being more palatable meant she'd find someone who would actually want her.

But now, with Noah at her side, the wedding would fall into one of the best times. She was sure of it.

She left Noah's house before he did, telling him they needed to arrive separately so that they could avoid any questions. In the car park she put on some make-up, and then looked down at the yellow floral dress she'd bought earlier that morning with Noah. She liked how bright it was against her skin. Liked that it made her feel like sunshine even when darkness still tumbled around inside her.

Taking a deep breath, she went to find her brother and future sister-in-law at the market. It was enthusiastically decorated for Christmas, and the prerequisite Father Christmas was in a cordoned-off area for kids to have their pictures taken with him. She smirked as 'Father Christmas' was handed a screaming child, before spotting Jaden and Leela at a large table.

'Ava.' Jaden got up and pulled her into a hug. 'Are you okay?'

'I'm fine,' she said brightly, before brushing a kiss on Leela's cheek. 'Like I told Mom and Dad *and* you on the phone last night, I was evacuated in time.'

'We wanted to come as soon as you called.'

'I know. But it made no sense. Your wedding venue is over an hour away, and it was late. I didn't want any of you driving when I was fine and I'd booked myself into a hotel. Again, I *told* you all this last night.'

'We were worried.'

She softened. 'I know, but I really am okay.'

'I heard the fire's changed direction, though,' Jaden said. She nodded. 'Have they told you when you'll get to move back?'

'Probably this evening.'

She said it even though it wasn't the truth—or at least she didn't know if it was. But she'd managed to temper their worry—though not as much as she'd first thought, she considered, looking at her brother. Still, convincing them to stay at the vineyard the night before had been no mean feat. They'd hovered over her since her wedding day—although, true to the tradition of her family, none of them had actually *asked* her about it.

But that didn't mean their concern for Ava had disappeared. And if she'd told them she'd had to go to the hospital—that Zorro had had to, too, and that he was still there—they'd have overreacted. She wasn't in the mood for that. Less so since she'd probably have to tell them *more* lies to hide the fact that she'd stayed at Noah's the night before.

If she couldn't move back to her house this evening she'd figure something out. But for now she had to distract her brother, so he wouldn't pry any more than he already had and become suspicious. Insults were the quickest—and easiest—way to do so.

'You need to get a life, Jaden. You can't be this worried about me after I told you I was fine.'

'Forgive me for caring.'

'Is that how you apologise to someone you care about?'

He rolled his eyes. 'I'm sorry that you're the most annoying little sister in the world.'

'Are we handing out apologies?' Noah asked, joining their group.

Jaden's face split into a grin and they did a little handshake and back pat, before her brother introduced Noah to Leela. Noah forewent another handshake and pulled Leela into a hug, and then they all settled at the table.

'So, where is it?' Noah asked.

'What?' Jaden replied, with a wider smile than Ava had seen on him in a long time.

'My apology?' When Jaden frowned, Noah said, 'I've heard there are some things about this wedding you haven't told me.'

Jaden's expression immediately dimmed, and Ava caught Leela's eye and gestured that they should get up. 'We're going to get some drinks,' she said, putting an arm through Leela's. 'We'll give you two a chance to catch up.'

'He feels bad about it,' Leela said when they were far away from the table. 'About the Tiff thing. About *your* thing, too.'

Ava blinked, and then let go of Leela's arm. This was the first time either Leela or Jaden had referred to their wedding being so close to the anniversary of Ava being jilted.

Ava had always assumed that it was out of a desire for self-preservation. That neither of them wanted to face Ava's potential wrath. But Ava had no desire to engage over it now. There was nothing any of them could do to change what was happening.

'I'm sure everything will be fine,' she said soothingly. 'Why don't you tell me about your trip? How did everything go?'

As she'd known it would, talking about the wedding distracted Leela. She went from serious to animated in seconds, and for a moment Ava wondered where Leela got her excitement from.

Ava had never been excited about her own wedding. Nervous and anxious, yes, but not excited. In fact, those nerves, that anxiety, had built and built until finally she'd been standing at the altar. She wondered now whether those emotions had been because she'd anticipated that Milo would leave her there.

Even now she couldn't figure it out. But she didn't think too hard about it. The memories of that day had gone on a shelf at the back of her mind—deep in her memory storage cupboard—along with the memories and emotions of Noah seven years ago. Memories and emotions that were best left alone.

She paid the bartender for their drinks, and

then she and Leela made their way back to the table. Things didn't seem too tense, but that didn't keep Ava from asking as she settled in next to Noah.

'All sorted?' she said under her breath as Jaden said something to Leela.

'About as much as it can be.'

'You have the moral high ground now,' she told him. 'But the moment he finds out I stayed at your place last night—'

'Don't even say it,' Noah muttered. 'He might hear, and I'm still begging for forgiveness for the last time something happened between us.'

'From him or from me?' she asked, before she could stop herself, and then she shook her head. 'Forget that. I don't have the energy to go down that road. No!' she said when he opened his mouth. 'If you try to talk to me about this I'm going to deduct points from you.'

'Against the rules.'

'There *are* no rules.'

'There's one rule now.' His eyes didn't leave hers. 'No deductions.'

'Fine.'

They stared at each other. But when it turned into something more than just defiance they both looked away.

Directly into the eyes of her brother.

CHAPTER NINE

'I TOLD YOU,' Ava said after a moment.

But the look on Jaden's face didn't change. It was almost as if he hadn't heard his sister.

Noah swallowed, and wondered whether it was too late to back out of the wedding. He didn't *have* to deal with these looks, or the reminder that Jaden had once thought Noah had taken advantage of Ava. Or that he sometimes believed that himself.

Ava nudged him with her elbow under the table, and then repeated her words. 'I told you, Noah. He was going to tell you.'

'Er…yeah. Sure…'

'What are you two talking about?' Jaden asked.

'Well, I ran into Noah yesterday,' Ava said easily. 'He was part of the team dispatched to the estate to deal with the fires. Anyway, I asked him about Tiff by mistake, and he didn't know.' She tilted her head. 'Even though he's been here for over *two weeks*, Jaden.'

'He was fighting fires,' Jaden said defensively. 'And why would you mention it anyway, if you weren't sure I'd told him?'

'Oh, I don't know.' She leaned forward. 'Maybe it was the surprise of seeing him at all, since you didn't even tell me he was here already.'

Jaden opened his mouth, but just then two other people joined their group. One Noah didn't recognise, though Jaden told him it was a colleague he'd grown close to. The other he recognised all too well.

He stood when the rest of them stood, and gave himself permission just to look at her. Ava was right; Tiff had dyed her hair. But other than that she looked the same as she had seven years before. Tall, smooth brown skin. Perfect features. One of the most beautiful women he'd ever seen.

But she'd changed the course of his life. He couldn't be drawn in by beauty any more.

'Noah,' she said, and surprised him with a hug. 'You look good.'

'Thank you.' He didn't bother telling her she looked good, too. She already knew. 'It's a...a surprise to see you.'

'But a *good* surprise?' she asked teasingly.

He opened his mouth to reply, but was interrupted by a snort coming from beside him. When he turned to look at Ava she widened her eyes in innocence. It immediately eased some of his tension.

'Ava,' Tiff said, in a tone that suggested she wasn't Ava's biggest fan. 'Such a treat to see you again.'

'Treat…inevitability…' Ava lifted her shoulders. 'To each his own, I guess.'

'Delightful, as always.'

Ava offered Tiff a smile, and he wondered if she thought the smile was sweet. It wasn't. It was terrifying. But it seemed to do the trick, because Tiff moved to sit at the opposite side of the table and not next to him, as he'd thought she'd initially intended to. Jaden's other groomsman—Ken—sat next to Ava.

'Sixty points,' Noah whispered as they took their seats again.

'Really?' Ava pulled her face. 'It hardly deserves that much. I was barely trying.'

'The rules are the rules.'

'Fair enough.' But her hand found his under the table and squeezed.

If someone had asked him how the afternoon would go after that moment, he wouldn't have been able to answer. Not coherently anyway.

He was much too aware of the two women at the table who represented such different things in his life.

He'd fallen so hard for Tiff that he wasn't surprised he still had the bruises to show for it. He'd met her during the second year of his photography course and had asked her out, considered getting his own place so that they could move in together, and had even been planning on proposing to her all in the space of a year. *One year.*

It hadn't seemed strange to him that their relationship had moved so fast. He'd only been thinking about that feeling in his chest when he was with her. How it made him feel invincible.

But he wasn't. Neither was their relationship. And when it had crashed and burned he'd seen nothing *but* how fast it had been. He'd seen that pace over his entire life, in his father's relationships—had witnessed it, had judged it—but he hadn't seen it in his own life. It was his biggest regret. And, though he'd never tell his father, his biggest failure.

His relationship with Tiff had changed him. Had changed the way he saw relationships. Changed the way he saw his father. How could he blame the man for falling so hard and fast when Noah had experienced it himself? So easily, too. It was worse because Noah knew his father's behaviour somehow linked back to what had happened with his mother.

But Noah's behaviour had come *before* he'd discovered Tiff cheating on him. He could only imagine what would have come after if he hadn't stopped himself.

He'd practised tight control in his dating life since then. He'd gone out occasionally, but he'd never invested too much of himself. He was too afraid of being sucked into that emotion again. Emotion that would lift him high enough that he'd *want* to experience it even after it had plunged him back to the ground.

That was how his father started his cycle; Noah refused to let it become his own.

And now, sitting opposite the woman who'd started it all…

It shook him more than he cared to admit.

As if sensing his thoughts, Ava bumped her shoulder against his. When he looked over she winked at him, and rolled her eyes in an exaggerated way before stifling a yawn. He smirked, and then full-out grinned when he felt a movement under the table and heard Ava hiss in response. Jaden sent her a pointed look—to go along with the kick under the table, Noah assumed—and again some of his tension faded.

Ava had always had the ability to do that. Which might have been why he'd ignored all his newly made resolutions the day he'd kissed her. There had been no control in that, and it had confused their relationship even more.

He'd had no idea what their relationship had been when they were growing up. He *still* didn't. He couldn't quite call them friends. Not in the way he'd call Jaden a friend. Nor was their relationship like that of family, no matter how much he'd tried to convince her—and himself—of that.

If it was, he was going to hell for all the improper thoughts he'd had about a family member. And so, just like he had before—before that kiss, at least—he would ignore the fact that those thoughts existed. Because although he couldn't define their relationship, he knew that it came with boundaries.

Unspoken ones at first, and then, after Jaden had caught them kissing, clearly outlined ones. In hard tones, loud volumes, and even louder disappointment.

He'd felt ashamed that he'd kissed her even as he'd done it. He hadn't needed Jaden to tell him he should have been. So when he'd moved away and hadn't said goodbye, he'd thought it for the best.

Except, he thought, remembering how Ava had looked when he'd told her he'd blocked her email address, maybe it hadn't been.

But it was in the past now. And that was where he needed to leave it all. His relationship with Tiff. The way he felt about relationships as a result. Whatever he'd once shared with Ava.

The way he was going to get through this wedding was to stay in the present. No matter how much the past called to him.

She'd sensed the change in him the moment her brother had joined them.

No, she thought. It had happened when her brother had caught them in that strangely intense look they'd shared. The easiness between them had slipped behind a barrier she only now realised had been there when they were younger, too. The kindness—the softness in his eyes when he'd look at her—had changed into something else. Something more...*polite*.

If she hadn't hated politeness before—the insincerity of it—Noah's reaction would have ensured it now.

And then Tiff had swooped in with her perfect beauty, and Ava had felt the Noah she'd been talking to—*engaging* with—since they'd reconciled slip even further away from her.

The tension had built inside her so much that at the first opportunity Leela gave them to leave the table, Ava jumped up and exited the tent that enclosed the market.

There was no one else in the field behind the tent, and it eased the weight that was on her chest. Until she heard the rustling of the grass behind her.

'Ava! Ava, wait!'

Her legs kept moving, though she wasn't completely sure why. Did they want distance from this stupid wedding and its stupid planning? Or were they running from the man who didn't have to do much to turn them into jelly?

'Hey,' Noah said, catching up to her.

She didn't stop.

'You okay?'

'Fine.'

'Ava? Ava, *stop*. Stop walking.'

She stopped—but not because he'd asked her to. They were far enough away from the market now that the live band who'd been singing songs about the festive season was muted. Plus, they'd reached the side of the field where a row of trees provided shade.

'What's going on?'

'Nothing. I just needed a break from…everything. The wedding.'

He studied her. 'Okay, fine. Let's pretend like I believe you. Which I don't.'

She didn't respond.

'Why did you agree to be in this wedding when you clearly don't want to be?'

'Have you ever tried refusing when a bride asks you to be a bridesmaid?'

He gave her a look.

'Or a groom asks you to be best man. Whatever. You know what I mean.' She took a breath. 'Not only did Leela ask me without any warning—I'm still working on forgiving my brother for *that*—she did it at Sunday lunch in front of both my family *and* hers. As much as I wanted to, I couldn't say no.'

'Surely they would have understood?'

'Surely Leela should have known that having her wedding exactly a year after mine *and* asking me to be in her bridal party wasn't a good idea? And yet here we are.'

He shoved his hands in his pockets, but Ava could have sworn he'd wanted to reach out to her first.

'I'm sorry.'

She waved a hand. 'Why should you apologise? You're in as much of a mess as I am.' She forced the next words out of her mouth. 'How was it? Seeing Tiff again?'

'Strange.' He kicked at the grass in front of him, watched as the dry golden-brown blades flattened. 'But fine.'

She snorted. 'Yeah, *right*.'

'If you can lie about what's going on, I can, too.'

'Touché.'

They stood like that for a few moments, and then Ava sighed. 'We should probably get back.'

'Why? So Leela can talk us into finding things to add to the wedding favours at the market?'

'Technically, that's what we're supposed to be doing now.'

'There are other people in the bridal party.'

'Yeah. And they've been doing the majority of the work for the past year. You weren't here, and I've been about as helpful as this conversation has been in working out our frustrations.'

He smiled. 'You have such an elegant way of describing things.'

'Of course I do. I'm a copywriter. I have to find wonderful ways of describing boring things all the time.'

'Should I be offended that you're calling me boring?'

'Not you. Or this conversation, really.'

She angled her body and he began to walk next to her at the sign. But their pace was slow, giving them plenty of time to avoid their duties.

'It's easier not to talk about things.'

'About the wedding?'

'About all of it.' She sighed. 'But even though I haven't spoken about it people still—'

She cut herself off. Revealing it to him felt as if she was confiding. She didn't *confide*. Confiding meant making herself vulnerable. Exposing herself, flaws and all. And she wouldn't do that when she was determined to keep those flaws to herself.

But she'd already said too much.

'People still treat you differently?'

She nodded. 'They treat me differently, and then they try to cover it up—which, again, makes them treat me differently. It's annoying. I mean, they were annoying before, but now they're *super*-annoying.'

'I know what you mean. Not about the annoying part,' he said when she shot him a look. 'At least not *entirely* about the annoying part. But, no, I meant about my father.'

Ava stopped herself from sucking in her breath; holding it in at the information he'd offered. Noah didn't ever speak about how his father's actions made him feel.

Or maybe he just didn't ever speak about it to you.

And why would he? she wondered in response to that inner voice. They'd never had the kind of relationship where they'd bare their souls to one another. Well, *she* had. But that was because she'd been young and foolish. Because she'd thought Noah was just as much her friend as he was Jaden's.

But their kisses had drawn lines in the sand. They'd managed to ignore the first line because they'd ignored the fact that the kiss had happened at all. And the second line...

Well, they'd never had to deal with that until now. She could feel that they were approaching it. But she wouldn't cross it.

If it was going to be crossed *he* would have to be the one who did it.

'It was worse when I was younger and didn't understand it. The only thing I knew was that whenever my father brought a new "friend" home, people would look at me in a certain way. The same way. When I was older I realised it was with sympathy.' He paused. 'They'd never say anything about it; they'd just give me sympathetic looks. And when he got married there were fake congratulations. When he divorced, fake consolation. It drove me mad.'

'I never realised.'

'Yeah, well... I became a pro at hiding it.' He gave her a slanted look. 'You, not so much.'

She laughed lightly, though it wasn't really funny. 'You'd be surprised.' But again, because that felt like confiding, she continued. 'It's never been my aim to hide it. Except maybe with my parents. They believe—' She cleared her throat when emotion stuck. 'They believe that I'm better than I am. I don't want to disappoint them. Not any more than I already have.'

Noah stopped, reaching out and grabbing her hand, forcing her to stop, too. 'You've *never* disappointed them.'

'You don't think their daughter being jilted in front of all their friends and family was a disappointment?' The words spilled from her lips unfiltered. 'You don't think realising there's something wrong with their daughter disappointed them?'

'Ava!' He said her name in both warning and surprise. 'Where is this coming from?'

'It's always been there,' she said flatly. 'I'm pretty sure you've experienced it yourself.'

CHAPTER TEN

NOAH HAD NO idea what Ava was talking about. Or where her words were coming from. Had he missed this side of her? Or had she just changed since he'd last seen her?

The latter, he thought, when his mind reminded him of who she'd been back then. Confident in her decisions. Brazen in her efforts. Fearless in her mistakes. The insecurities she was showing him now had come after. And the thought of it had his blood boiling.

'Who *is* this man?'

She blinked. 'What?'

'The man who left you. Who is he?'

'Why?'

'Because I'm going to kill him for doing this to you.'

She stared at him, her hand slackening in his. 'I don't—I don't understand.'

'The last time I saw you, you weren't this person. *He* did this to you.' The venom in his voice surprised him.

She shook her head. 'Don't be an idiot, Noah.'

'He broke your heart and made you doubt yourself.'

'He didn't break my heart.'

But she didn't say he hadn't made her doubt herself. The absence of those words echoed loudly between them.

'I'm going to make it painful,' Noah said after a moment.

'Noah, stop it.' She let out a harsh breath. 'It doesn't matter. It's over.'

'And you're fine with being like this now?'

'I've always been like this.'

'This is *not* who you've always been.'

'How would you know?'

'Because I know you.'

'You *knew* me. Or you thought you did.'

'No.'

'Yes. Because *I* didn't really know my-self then either.' She pulled her hand from his completely. 'It's been seven years, Noah. Seven years and things have happened and I've changed. I've got to know who I really am. It has nothing to do with him.'

She walked ahead now, leaving him staring at her back. He had no idea what had just happened. He didn't know where her fierce

response had come from. Nor the fierce protectiveness in his chest.

He hoped what she'd said wasn't true. Knew
that there was enough of the old Ava there to
give that hope life. Because if there wasn't he'd
have to wonder if he'd had anything to do with
it. If his walking away—walking away after
kissing her—had been part of what had caused
her to change so drastically.

But that wasn't possible. It was too vain for
him even to think that. And it told him he
needed to re-evaluate the power he'd thought
he had in a relationship he couldn't even define.

It bothered him for the rest of the afternoon.
Bothered him more than having the woman
who'd broken his heart sit across from him.
More than having to listen to her make conversation as they went through the market, trying
to find things to add to the favours to give the
Keller wedding more of a festive feel.

He ignored Tiff for the most part, and
breathed a sigh of relief when she seemed to
get the picture. But there was no relief from the
situation with Ava. And by the time Leela gave
them updated information about the rehearsal

dinner, happening in a few days' time, he still hadn't figured it out.

'Are you coming?' Jaden interrupted his thoughts.

'Where?'

'To my place for drinks.' Jaden frowned, making it clear that Noah had missed the invitation. 'To end the day.'

I can't think of anything I want to do less.

He didn't say it. Instead he looked at Ava, and she gave an imperceptible shake of the head. She wasn't going. And since she was still staying with him—he assumed—he'd pass, too.

'Nah. I'm still not feeling great after the fire yesterday. I should probably get some rest or I might be out for longer than I want to be.'

'What fire?' Tiff asked.

'It's a little too late to be concerned about my well-being,' he replied flatly. Being out of sorts with Ava had destroyed his filter. He felt bad almost immediately, and added a weak, 'But thanks for asking.'

'You sure you're okay?' Jaden asked as his frown deepened. 'Should I come over to your place for a catch-up?'

'No,' he said—a little too intensely, he thought, when he saw the surprise on Jaden's face. When he saw the smirk on Ava's. 'No, it's fine. We'll catch up another time. Go have fun.'

Giving him a suspicious look, Jaden nodded. 'Ava?'

'Oh, no. I can't imagine anything more terrible.'

She gave her brother a smile, and Noah saw Jaden's annoyance soften.

'But thanks for asking.'

She aimed a sweet, slightly mocking smile at Noah, and he couldn't help the way his lips curved in return. But when Jaden narrowed his eyes at them Noah sobered immediately. Thankfully Jaden didn't say anything about it, and then he and Ava were alone.

'I thought that would never end.'

'Me, too.' He paused, and was about to say something about what had happened between them earlier when she spoke.

'Forty points for that jibe against Tiff. You could have got fifty, but then you said thank you and it kind of spoilt it for me.'

'I felt bad.'

'You shouldn't have. She broke your heart.'

'Yeah, but we were kids.'

'You're defending her? After what she did?'

He quirked an eyebrow. 'How much do you know about that?'

'Nothing.' Her cheeks went pink.

'Jaden told you, didn't he?'

'No.' When he didn't reply, she sighed. 'I swear he didn't.' Then she mumbled something.

'What?'

She mumbled again.

'Ava,' he said exasperatedly.

'*You* told me, okay? Inadvertently. That night you and Jaden were sitting out on the balcony, talking about it.'

He remembered the night in question. It had been the day after he'd found Tiff half-naked with another man in the driveway of her house. He'd worked through most of his shock at that point. Mainly because Tiff had tried to explain it away—although why she'd even tried made no sense to him—and he'd accepted that things were over.

He'd been in the first stage of trying to figure out what that meant when he'd told Jaden.

'Where were you hiding?'

Though her cheeks darkened, she answered him. 'On the veranda underneath the balcony. Pretending to read a romance novel so my parents thought I was being productive. Which I *was* being. At first.' She wrinkled her nose. 'But you weren't really keeping your voices down.'

'It was a private conversation,' he said sternly.

'I know. I'm sorry.'

He waited a beat. 'No, you're not.'

'No, I'm not.' She lifted a shoulder. 'It's the reason we can have this conversation, isn't it?'

'You say that as if it's a *good* thing.'

'Well, I told you that my fiancé left me. Think of it as an equal exchange of information, if you like.'

'I'm not sure I do.' But then he shrugged. 'It was a long time ago. Much further back than what happened to you.' He paused. 'You'll get over it.'

'But it changes you. It changes you in general, I mean,' she added hastily when he frowned.

'It wasn't too bad in my case.'

She narrowed her eyes, but then her features relaxed. 'Sure.' She paused. 'Do you want to get out of here? I mean, it's pretty and all, but the live Christmas jingles are getting to me. And Father Christmas keeps looking at every pretty woman who passes in a way that's threatening to ruin my childhood memories.'

'Yeah, fine.'

But he didn't trust the change in her mood.

It was early evening as they headed for the car park, and the light was dim enough that the market's Christmas lights had been switched on. He couldn't deny it gave things a festive feel. The kind he'd only ever really felt in South Africa.

It was strange, considering he'd been all over the world. He'd spent Christmases in America, in the UK, in other African countries. He'd seen Thanksgiving and snow—things that made it clear Christmas was on its way.

Comparatively, there wasn't much in South Africa that did that. But there was a *feeling* here. When the Christmas carols started playing in stores late in November. When the decorations went up and Christmas trees could be found in the strangest public places around the country. When Christmas lights went on and families got together.

The feeling was so much more special now, since he'd been away for such a long time. And it made him realise how bad it must have been for his father to be away from South Africa at Christmas time.

Kirk loved Christmas. Once, when Noah had asked why, his father had told him he wanted to make sure Noah got the experiences he hadn't had growing up. But Noah knew that wasn't it. Not when his father's zeal for Christmas seemed to have started the year after Noah's mother had died. And since then Noah and his father had never spent a Christmas apart.

So maybe it wasn't so much Christmas in South Africa that Kirk loved as it was spending time with *Noah* during Christmas. Which was the kind of long-term commitment that Noah hadn't seen in any of his father's other relationships.

Noah, a voice in his head said in warning. It sounded disappointed, and it reminded him of how Ava had said his name when he'd mentioned his father's disregard for marriage earlier. It stung now, as it had then, but almost immediately resistance surged inside him.

He couldn't just *forget* how Kirk's relationships had affected him. How they had caused him to have the mixed-up belief that because of his father's relationships he'd attract the same kind in his own life. How a part of him didn't believe it was all that bizarre, since his first serious relationship had ended with him being cheated on just as his father had been.

'It's not that bad.'

He blinked. 'What?'

'The lights.' She looked back at the market, at the trees that surrounded it, the lights that adorned them. 'It's quite festive.'

'I agree.'

'So why are you scowling?'

'I was thinking about my father.'

He heard her unspoken question and realised it was the second time he'd brought his father up with her that night.

'He loves Christmas.'

'Yes.'

He lifted his eyebrows. 'You know?'

'For as long as I've known you, I've known Kirk loves Christmas. And we're friends now, remember? I decorate his tree with him.'

He hid his surprise. 'Do you make him buy food, too?'

'Yes, actually.'

She smiled at him and he angled his body towards her, as if to catch that smile.

'But the whole thing is much more successful with him. We actually decorate the tree, for instance.'

'Isn't that what we're going to do at home now?'

She gave him a strange look, and he realised his body was now completely facing hers. He also realised he'd spoken about 'home' as if he had one. As if the years he'd been a vagrant, photographing anything from fauna to civil wars, hadn't been an attempt to figure out whether he *wanted* a home.

'I should probably find somewhere else to stay.'

'Or you could stop resisting my help and just come to my house until you can go back to your own,' he said. 'You can't stay with your family unless you want to explain to them where you stayed last night. And we've already been through why a hotel won't work.'

She turned to face him, the distance between their bodies minimal now, and suddenly his thoughts stepped into dangerous territory. *Forbidden* territory, only ventured into once before. No, twice, he thought as Ava's eyes met his.

He didn't give much thought to the first time they'd kissed. Ava had told him she'd wanted to know what it felt like; he'd agreed. Because if it hadn't been him it would have been someone else. That had been a given, but he'd known what kind of mood she'd been in that night. She wouldn't have cared about *who* she'd got to kiss her.

At least with him she'd been safe.

He'd brushed off the stirrings of his body back then. Told himself it was just hormones. Sexual frustration. And when she'd given him a bright smile, declaring it had never happened as she bounced off, he'd set it aside.

But now he remembered those stirrings. Because they were back, and more acute now than they'd been then. More acute now than they'd been when he'd kissed her the second time. The time that had nothing to do with familiarity or safety. The time that had been about danger and unsafe territory.

Just like now.

'Fine. But only because I need to help you with your tree. Because I owe you.' Her voice was husky.

'You don't owe me anything, Avalanche.' He lifted a hand and brushed at the hair curling over her forehead. 'If you did, you've already repaid me.'

'No,' she denied.

She took a step closer to him, though he didn't think she was aware of it. At least not fully. Just as he wasn't fully aware of his other hand lifting and resting on her waist.

'How could I have?' Her voice was breathless now. 'I did nothing.'

'You saved me from Father Christmas and the elves throwing up in my house. You helped set up my tree. Or you will. And you saved me from the humiliation and emotion of seeing my cheating ex-girlfriend again.'

'I didn't save you from anything.'

'You did,' he said, and felt the mood shift from flirtatious to serious. To intense.

The air sizzled around them.

'Noah...'

She said his name on a sigh; half defeat, half frustration. But there was more in her tone, and he couldn't quite figure it out. Because he couldn't, he took a step back.

Before he could speak, her phone rang.

'The vet,' she said, her face tightening into an expression he almost felt in his stomach. But her voice was steady when she told him, 'I'll meet you at your place later.'

She'd answered the phone before he could reply.

'I'm *so* sorry, my sugar plum,' Ava murmured to Zorro as she snuggled him. She could feel his displeasure, but he didn't claw his way out of her embrace. Which he would have done if he hadn't missed her just a tiny bit.

Eventually she let go of him, setting him on her lap and waiting to see what he wanted to do. He gave her a look that confirmed he wasn't happy, but settled into a sitting position. She supposed it was the lesser of two evils. He didn't want to go back into his carrier, and the rest of her car seemed equally unappealing. She had no doubt he'd run far away from her the moment they got home.

It took her a second to realise that she wasn't sure *when* they'd get home—she hadn't heard anything about the state of her house yet—and she dropped her head back against the headrest and evaluated her life choices.

She'd managed to call the vet that morning, but the receptionist had said the vet had been called in to an emergency operation and would return her call that afternoon. She'd completely forgotten about Zorro after that. She'd been too enamoured with her childhood crush. Too busy playing games with him that would have no winner. Not if she kept going the way that she was.

The moment they'd shared as they'd left the market had been a clear sign that going back to Noah's would be a mistake. But her options were limited—just as Noah had pointed out. No family, no hotel. And the fire *had* changed direction. Surely it wouldn't be long before she'd be able to go back home? It wouldn't kill her to stay at Noah's for one more night.

Maybe they could just focus on decorating

the Christmas tree. And they could keep the conversation neutral, like talking about their jobs.

But then she remembered what had happened when she'd needed to take the angel off the top of the Christmas tree. And how talking about her writing career earlier had led to her almost confiding in him.

She let out a breath. She didn't have much choice, and she could hardly stay parked at the end of Noah's road for ever. So, like her cat, Ava chose the lesser evil and made the short trip back to the house of temptation.

CHAPTER ELEVEN

'Everything okay with Zorro?'

'See for yourself.'

Ava lowered herself to her haunches, opened the door of the carrier, and out came the ugly cat. He immediately drew himself up as he looked around, realising he wasn't at his own house. Noah almost held his breath when the cat aimed its creepy, unblinking stare at him, but quickly realised that was ridiculous and let out the air in his lungs.

If only he'd been able to shake off the unsettled feeling he'd had since leaving the market as easily.

'I'm going to be honest with you. I'm not entirely sure what I should be looking for.'

She laughed softly, almost hesitantly. 'The vet said he's fine. He's on anti-inflammatories, but they didn't think it was serious enough for antibiotics. Which once again proves how much I owe you.'

'You don't owe me anything.'

Zorro gave a loud meow, and Ava quirked a brow. 'Humour me.'

'Fine,' he said, mostly because he was tired of arguing. 'What will it take for you to think we're even?'

'A flat hundred points?'

Not expecting that, he leaned forward. 'I'm not sure I can accept. This isn't a part of the bet.'

'So let's *make* it a part of the bet.'

'No,' he said after a moment. 'That blurs the lines too much.'

'It blurs the lines of the imaginary game you and I set up?'

He shrugged, and she let out a breath.

'How about supper, then?'

'I feel *so* appreciated.'

'Noah.'

He smirked. 'I have to eat.'

'Yes, you do.' She went to the kitchen, opened a cupboard door. And then did the same for each of the other cupboards. 'There's nothing here.'

'There are eggs.'

'Nothing,' she repeated. 'How do you feed yourself?'

'The deli. Plus, there are still croissants from this morning left over.'

'I'm not feeding you croissants for supper.' There was a beat before she continued. 'Watch Zorro. I'm going to the shop. I'll be back before you can get weird about babysitting a cat.'

True to her word, she left before he could protest.

'Your owner has a habit of leaving before I can argue with her,' he told the cat after a moment. 'Should I interpret that as a sign of her approach to life?'

The cat jumped onto his kitchen counter and gave him a level stare, as if to say, *You're on your own here, buddy. I'm not saying a word about her.*

'Loyalty,' he commented. 'I guess I can respect that.'

Not wanting to examine how he felt about calling a cat loyal, he got himself a beer. His body groaned when he lowered himself on the couch shortly after, and he realised it hadn't entirely been a lie when he'd told Jaden he needed rest.

His throat felt significantly better, though there was still the occasional cough. But he'd survive, he thought, and brought the beer to his lips.

He just wasn't sure he'd survive having Ava stay another night.

Things had become uncomfortable at the market. Probably before that, he realised, remembering how she'd responded to his 'I blocked your emails' news. It annoyed him, but there wasn't much he could do about it. Talking about what had happened would only make things worse. And clearly ignoring it did, too. But he had no energy to try and figure out how to make things better. So he'd let things sort themselves out.

He set the beer on the table, kicked off his shoes and made himself comfortable on the couch, switching the TV on. With some undemanding Christmas movie playing, he settled back and told himself to relax.

Clearly he'd listened to himself, too, because when he opened his eyes again there were people on the TV screen he didn't recognise from before, and his house smelled of an enticing array of spices.

He shifted, and then frowned when he felt pressure on his chest. When he saw why, he wasn't sure how he'd missed that Zorro was sitting on his chest. The cat was giving him that blank, staring look, and this time it seemed to say, *Sit up. I dare you.*

Not appreciating being taunted by a cat, Noah

shifted, and Zorro gave him a look of disgust—or disappointment—before gracefully leaping off his chest.

'Oh, you're awake,' Ava said as she moved a pot from the stove to the counter.

'I didn't realise I'd been asleep.'

'I figured. Your beer was only half-drunk when I got back from the shop.'

'How long ago was that?' he asked, standing before doing a quick stretch. He felt his body crack, heard it sigh, and then shook his arms out.

When he met Ava's eyes again, she blushed.

'Not too long,' she said, though it sounded forced. 'An hour? Hour and a half?'

'I must have been tired.'

'Clearly.' She paused. 'You didn't sleep well last night. Why?'

'Sometimes a fire sits with you.'

'Did this one sit because of me?'

He was going to deny it, but then figured he had no reason to lie. 'Partly. But it's never easy to think about the people who are going to lose their homes. And the damage to the area.' He shrugged. 'Part of the job.'

'I didn't realise.' Her expression twisted in

sympathy. 'Why would you want to volunteer, then?'

'You're asking me that *now*?' he said with a smirk. 'I did the training when I was eighteen. You know that.'

'Yeah, I guess I'm just delayed in asking about it.' She took plates from his cupboard. 'Doesn't change the fact that I want to know.'

He grinned at her sass. 'Sure. My dad told me to find something I could do to help people. We used to make sandwiches and give them to the homeless every Tuesday. Every second Thursday we'd volunteer at the soup kitchen.'

She frowned. 'Really? Why didn't I know that?'

'It's not something we advertised. It wasn't about that for my dad. And he taught me that, too.'

'So even though you could afford to donate to charities who did things like that, you chose to do it yourselves?'

'We did both. It's part of the responsibility when you have more than others.'

He lifted a shoulder, though it felt as if he carried weight there. But he ignored it—just as he ignored the guilt he felt at the resentment he held for his father when Kirk had made such an effort raising him.

'In any case, after the fires in Kayamandi we were at the station, trying to figure out how we could help, and I heard one of the guys saying they wished they had more volunteers. I knew it was something I could do.'

'Sounds like a noble decision,' she noted quietly. 'Though you were so scrawny back then.'

He laughed, unoffended. 'I guess. Things started to change after I took the training. I tried to do more.'

'And then you left.'

Was that a hitch he heard in her voice? 'Yeah, but I trained as much as I could while I was away. Found stations to volunteer at if I stayed anywhere long enough. When I got back, the station put me through the final test again and brought me in when I passed.'

He accepted the fresh beer she handed him before dishing up their food.

'They needed as many hands as they could get.'

'Volunteer firefighter, silent philanthropist, photojournalist...'

She gave him a plate and he realised why what she'd made smelled that good. Biriyani. *Biriyani*.

'That's quite the CV, Mr Giles.'

'Yeah, but it doesn't include the ability to

make biriyani.' He inhaled appreciatively. 'How did you manage to make this so quickly?'

She laughed. 'I became a pro when I realised I didn't care for the commitment of more than two hours for cooking. It probably doesn't taste as good as those ones, but you'll survive.'

He took a mouthful and groaned. 'This is just as good as any other I've tasted.'

She reached over the counter and patted his cheek. 'Oh, poor, naïve Noah. I do appreciate your inexperience.'

He snorted, but didn't reply. Not only because the food was genuinely amazing, but because her touch had seared his skin. And he couldn't do anything about it. Couldn't say anything about it. He was sure that if he did the easiness they'd somehow got back would disappear.

'I'm sure your dad is looking forward to having you around for the next few weeks.'

'Yeah.' He frowned. 'But it isn't for a few weeks.'

'No? He told me—' She broke off when he gave her a look. Again, a pretty blush stained her cheeks. 'He likes talking about you.'

'Does he? How much?'

'Every time I visit.'

Needing time to digest that information, he

ate more food, and then took his time drinking his beer.

'I know we've spoken about it, but this friendship you have with my dad is weird.'

She laughed softly and settled next to him with her own food. But she didn't start eating. Instead, she ran her fork over the rice, ruffling it as she did so, over and over.

'I used to think so, too. And so does Jaden. And my parents.'

'They're probably worried he's going to rob the cradle. What?' he asked when she gave him an unhappy look. 'It's happened before. It'll happen again.'

'He's *lonely*, Noah. Your mother died when you were four. Can you imagine the loneliness that follows losing the love of your life *and* having to raise a four-year-old by yourself?'

'That loneliness has nothing to do with my mother dying.'

'Of course it does. Your father's love for your mother—'

'Made him weak.' Bitterness controlled his tongue. 'She cheated on him and he forgave her, even though I know how much she hurt him. That's when the real loneliness started.'

He ran a hand over his mouth, then pressed it to the counter.

'And then she died, and he started jumping from one relationship to another. But that had nothing to do with loneliness. He was—*is*—just running from his weakness. From her. From the memory of her.'

When she didn't respond he looked over at her, and winced when he saw her face.

'You didn't know.'

She shook her head slowly.

'I'm sorry, I thought—'

'Don't,' she interrupted. 'You have nothing to apologise for.'

'I thought… You're friends with him… Or Jaden…' He didn't know what he was saying. Or why he still felt as if he needed to apologise.

'Jaden wouldn't have told me,' she said after a long pause. 'He wouldn't have broken your trust like that. And your father…' She took another pause. 'My friendship with your father started because I didn't want to…to talk about things.'

She cleared her throat.

'About being left at the altar. About how it messed with—' She broke off, gave a quick shake of her shoulders. 'My point is that your father never asked me about any of it. And, yeah, neither did *my* family, but your father's silence about it didn't come with expectations. He didn't… He didn't *need* me to pretend that I was fine when I wasn't.'

'But your family did?'

'It was better for us all if I pretended. That way they could move on with their lives and I could…*deal* with things.' Her face tightened, but she continued. 'And even though your father didn't ask me anything, he let me ask *him* things. And he answered, even though some of my questions were inappropriate.'

His heart thudded. 'What did you ask him?'

'How he could deal with the failures. With the broken relationships. With the brokenness.' She lifted her hands and he knew she was referring to herself. As if *she* were broken. 'He told me I needed to move on. Move forward. And that was it. That was about as deep as we got. He wouldn't have told me about it either.'

He didn't reply. Tried to process what she was saying.

'I think,' she said slowly, 'that, for him, moving on—moving forward—meant pretending like your mother didn't cheat.' She hesitated on the last word. 'I'm sorry.'

'Don't be. It makes sense.'

And because it did, he couldn't find the words to break the silence that fell over them. He ate the rest of his dinner, but didn't taste it. And then he excused himself and went to do the dishes.

A part of him knew that his feelings about his father were irrational. And that somewhere in those feelings there was an anger he'd transferred to his father after his mother had died. After he'd realised the truth of what she'd done, of what he'd seen. After his father had confirmed it.

Because how could he have been upset with his mother? His life had gone on in the same way it had before he'd seen his mother with another man. Even when, as an adult, he'd thought back to the few memories he had of before she'd died, Noah couldn't remember his parents acting any differently because of what had happened. It had only been after her death that things had changed. And he couldn't blame her for that.

But he did blame his father.

All Noah had seen growing up had been a steady influx of women in his father's life. Some stayed longer than others. Some were kinder than others. And sure, those who'd been kinder *had* stayed for longer.

But as the father of a young child, shouldn't his father have protected him from witnessing that? From experiencing the instability? From the consequences Noah now saw in his own life because of it?

Or had he wanted his father to protect him from what his mother had done?

He paused as the thought stumped him. As it had him wondering if his father wasn't the only one running from the memory of his mother. Whether Noah's stance on relationships was just as much because of his mother's cheating as it was because of his father's behaviour.

Was *he* weak, too?

'Noah?' Ava said softly, and he started when he saw her standing in the kitchen with him. 'Are you okay?'

'Fine,' he lied, though he didn't think he did it particularly well. Not when the uneasiness in his chest was reflected in his tone.

Had he been judging his father too harshly?

There was a long silence as she studied him. As he dried his hands off to give them something to do because her looking at him made him restless. And then she stepped forward and slipped her hands around his waist, laying her head on his chest.

In that simple movement the war inside him settled. As if her body against his—her body in his arms—had brokered some kind of peace treaty. Pieces mended that he hadn't known were broken before. And one particular piece—one he'd known about but had ignored—clicked into place.

He couldn't run from her. He'd never been able to.

He tightened his arms around her and then stepped back, afraid of what he might do now that he'd allowed himself to acknowledge that he felt something for her. Afraid of what it meant that he'd let himself acknowledge it *now,* after discovering that his relationship fears extended more deeply than he'd thought.

It had thrown everything he knew about himself, about their relationship, into a hurricane he could feel inside him. And facing it would bring that hurricane's destruction into his life. Into their lives.

He couldn't do it. He wouldn't.

She sensed the shift before she saw it. On his face. In his body. His eyes.

But then, what did she expect? He'd just told her his mother had cheated on his father. And *she'd* told him that maybe his father had chosen not to remember that fact so that he could move on with his life. So that he could move on from Noah's *mother*. So that he could move on *with other women.*

Milo was right; she *did* have a knack for saying the worst things at the worst times. It had been one of the many things he'd told her when he'd listed the faults which made her unsuitable for marriage. Faults that had had her remembering every single failure in her life and how they'd somehow been a result of those faults.

'You're too honest.'
'You say the wrong things all the time.'
'You make light of everything.'
'You're so prickly.'

It sickened her that she still heard his voice in her head. That the insecurity she'd felt since then was almost a daily occurrence. But the doubt didn't leave her just because she was annoyed it had come courtesy of her ex. Though she wished it didn't have her regretting simple things, like offering someone she cared about a hug because she wanted to comfort him.

To avoid thinking about it, she walked back

around the counter and forced herself to finish her meal. She handed Noah the dish once she was done, and as he washed it, she went over to the couch where Zorro had made himself comfortable.

But her thoughts still buzzed in her head, like a fly caught in a room looking for an escape.

Suddenly determined to quieten them, she stood and got her phone. She scrolled to the appropriate song, linked her phone to Noah's Bluetooth speakers, and a few seconds later Christmas carols filled the room.

Zorro looked up in confusion at the sound, and Ava's lips twitched when, seconds later, she saw the same expression mirrored on Noah's face.

'Care to explain?' he asked as he joined her in the living room.

'We are *not* going to get sucked into the drama of this wedding and this season and our pasts,' she told him fiercely. 'So we're going to decorate this tree and have fun doing it.'

CHAPTER TWELVE

IT *WAS* FUN.

He hadn't expected it to be. He'd expected tension after their conversation. After their hug. But it was almost as if Ava had closed the door on anything that might have prevented them from having a good time. And somehow he found himself following suit, refusing to let himself dwell on the darkness of his realisations.

She'd always had the ability to do that. To make things seem…lighter. And whether that was because she joked about them or because she put her unique brand of I-don't-care on it, she never failed to make him feel better.

Which, he supposed, was part of his problem.

'Do you remember that year Jaden went through his goth phase?' Ava handed him a twinkling ball and pointed to where she wanted him to hang it on the tree.

'I do. Fondly. Although, as soon as it was

over he vehemently denied it had ever happened.'

'And we'd believe him,' she said, eyes twinkling, 'if it weren't for photographic evidence.'

'You have *photos*?'

'*So* many photos.' She handed him another ball, waving her hand to indicate that he could put it anywhere. 'The goth one is my favourite. Especially because it happened over Christmastime, and the contrast between our Christmas tree and Jaden's all-black clothing is hilarious. Well, that and the fact that I get to use it for my slideshow at the rehearsal dinner.'

His eyes widened. 'They're letting you do a *slideshow*?'

'*Letting* is not quite the word. I'd say forcing.' She stretched up to put the last of the ornaments at the top of the tree, revealing the smooth skin at her belly. Noah swallowed.

'Leela wanted to include me. Again, I couldn't exactly say no. The upside is neither could Jaden. Though he's begged me to keep it "appropriate".'

'Which, of course, you'll ignore.'

'Of course,' she agreed, smiling winningly at him.

His heart pattered. 'An unfair advantage for our game.'

Something tightened on her face, but then she relaxed. 'Perhaps. But you have your best man's speech, so—'

'Oh, no.' He groaned.

'Oh, no?' she repeated with a smile, and finished putting tinsel around the base of the tree. 'Did you forget? Please tell me you forgot. It would make my night.'

'I *did* forget.' He rubbed a hand over his face, and then sank down into a chair. When he felt it dip behind him, he realised he'd almost sat on the cat. 'Sorry,' he said absentmindedly, and then shook his head. 'Jaden didn't tell me.'

'I'm sure he didn't think he had to. It's a well-known responsibility of the best man. Which you should have known, considering...' She trailed off with a wrinkled nose, but he couldn't tell if it was because of their earlier discussion or because she was making fun of him.

'Yeah, well, my dad didn't once ask me to make a speech. He must have known I might have said something...unfiltered.'

'Or maybe he just didn't care about tradition.'

She smiled, and he realised it was a peace offering. An apology of sorts in case she'd offended him. But other than the fact that he had to take a moment to figure out whether she was right—she *did* seem to understand his father better than he did—he hadn't been offended. And she should have known that.

'Look, I don't want us to tiptoe around each other because of—' he waved a hand '—everything. My relationship with my father is complicated. More so, I think, because I've never told him how I feel. About what happened with my mother or about his relationships after.'

There was pulse in the air, and Noah's heart dropped.

'I thought you said you didn't talk about deep things,' he said.

'I also told you we speak about you a lot,' she replied sympathetically. 'I mean, I might be wrong, but he's always spoken as if he knows about your disapproval. At least about his relationships after your mother.' She paused. 'Again, I know this is probably really weird for you, and I'm sorry. In fact, if I'd known you'd be coming back and we'd be having this conversation, maybe I wouldn't have become his friend.'

'You didn't think I was coming back?'

'You didn't,' she pointed out. 'For seven years you didn't come back.'

He straightened in his seat. 'It bothered you?' When she shook her head, looked away, his heart ached. 'It *hurt* you.'

'It's not… I'm fine. I'm *fine*,' she said again as he stretched out and took her hand, pulling her towards him so that she could sit down next to him.

He put his arm around her waist—gently, loosely—so that if she wanted she could pull away from him.

'I didn't realise. I should have, but I didn't.'

'Why should you have known? We weren't friends.'

'But we were *something*.' Unable to resist, he lifted a hand and cupped her cheek. 'I don't have the words to describe it, so I'll settle for that. Something. We were something.'

'Something?' she repeated, and lifted a hand over his. 'It's describes this—us—perfectly.'

He smiled, and then felt it fade. 'I am sorry. I shouldn't have blocked you. I should have tried to contact you.'

'Why didn't you?'

His hand fell to her lap and her own followed quickly, tangling with his. As if she wanted to tell him that her question hadn't been an accusation. As if she wanted him to know that her hurt didn't matter.

And, because it did, he answered her truthfully. 'I was scared. I was scared that I'd messed it up with that kiss.'

'How could you have messed it up when it had been fine before? After the first kiss.'

'Because before—' He sucked in a breath. 'Before you were just sixteen. You didn't know any better, and I… I made excuses.'

Her eyes widened, and when he realised how deep a hole he'd dug himself he tossed the shovel aside and dived in.

'I told myself anything I had to to make sure things wouldn't change—just like we agreed.'

'And the second time?'

'The second time… Well, the second time, there wasn't an opportunity for excuses. There was just accusation. Just guilt.'

Her hand tightened, and it felt as if she were pulling away from him. But he held on.

'It was easier to feel that way than to feel something else, Ava. And I was scared of losing my friendship with Jaden.'

'But what about *me*?'

He couldn't answer that question. Didn't know if he could tell her that his guilt had been about more than just his friendship with Jaden.

It had been about taking advantage of her. Taking his broken heart out on her.

'I made a mistake,' he said softly.

'It wasn't a mistake. It was a choice. You made a choice.'

When she lifted her eyes to his, what he saw there stole his breath.

'Just like you chose to cut all contact with me.' She blew out a breath. 'You chose Jaden. I don't blame you for that. At least, I try not to.'

'I couldn't stay in touch with you and keep believing it was a mistake.'

He'd surprised himself with that, and when silence followed his words, he didn't know how to break it. Eventually she nodded, and then patted his hand with hers.

'Come on,' she said, her voice sounding as if she were fighting for the easy tone. 'We still have to put the angel on top of the tree.'

'Sure,' he said, determination lighting inside him. 'But first, I need to make another decision. We both do, actually.'

'What are you talking about?'

'I want to kiss you, Ava,' he said softly. 'But because it's going to complicate our lives, without a doubt, I need you to make that decision with—'

She pressed her lips to his.

* * *

She'd heard nothing more after Noah had said he wanted to kiss her. Which was probably why she was still kissing him, even though somewhere vaguely in her mind she knew he'd been warning her about something.

But who cared when his lips were on hers? When this gorgeous, sexy, *beautiful* man was kissing her?

In that moment she forgot that she'd been left at the altar. She forgot that even on her best days the fact that she had been left at the altar took something from her.

But not now. Oh, no, not now.

Now she was thinking that she was whole again. That Milo had been a fool to leave her. That *he* had been in the wrong. That *he'd* been the reason things hadn't worked out.

Because it was hard to think of herself as anything less than perfect when Noah Giles was kissing her.

He was the kind of kisser who did everything intentionally. Every touch of his tongue, every movement of his lips—all intentional. And all with the intention of making her—Ava Keller, the woman he was kissing—feel as if she were the only woman in the entire world.

She let him sweep her away with it. Let herself enjoy the way he knew which plunge of his tongue would give her goosebumps. Let herself lean into the way his fingers brushed over her body, the way his hands kneaded and squeezed.

She felt powerful when she heard him moan. Felt a healing warmth pool in her heart just as she felt it pool low in her stomach. She didn't complain when he pulled away from her mouth and pressed kisses on her jaw, on the slope of her neck. Heard herself moan when his mouth claimed hers again with a passion—a *need*—she didn't think she'd ever felt from a man before.

This kiss was nothing like the ones they'd shared before. It wasn't inquisitive, nor desperate, though there was both curiosity and desperation in the mating of their lips now. But the overriding emotion Ava felt as she kissed Noah was the sense that it was *right*. That this was where she *belonged*.

It was a terrible thing to feel. And it would no doubt keep her awake long after it had ended. But for now, in this moment, she let herself feel right. She let herself feel whole. And when he shifted and pressed his body over hers she let herself be seduced.

* * *

'We probably shouldn't—'

Ava cut him off by pulling his head back to hers, and Noah smiled against her mouth, letting her kiss him.

He didn't want to be the one who stopped them. Knew that if he did he'd regret it. But then, he thought, maybe he'd regret it anyway. More intensely once he realised that he *was* kissing her. That he was *enjoying* kissing her. That he wanted nothing more than to *keep* kissing her.

'Ava,' he said with a sigh, leaning his forehead against her. 'This is turning into something that—'

'Something that both of us want and one of us *desperately* needs to get out of her head?'

He chuckled lightly, and pressed a peck to her lips. 'Yes. Both of us for both of those things.'

'Then why are you stopping?'

'Because it's too fast.'

'Hmm…' she said, and shifted under him.

He got up, and for the first time noticed the cat watching them from the opposite coach. He wasn't even sure when Zorro had moved. He'd been too…involved.

'Fast used to be your pace.'

'And look where *that* got me.' *And my fa-*

ther. 'So I suppose the more important question at this point it why you're so determined to go fast.'

'I'm not—'

'Ava,' he interrupted gently.

She sighed. 'Maybe I think that if we go fast we'll outrun the reasons this is a bad idea. Or forget how poorly it could turn out.'

He stared at her, and then laughed. 'Well, you *do* have a point.'

Her mouth curved. 'I generally seem to.'

'And yet you still doubt yourself,' he said. 'You shouldn't.'

She opened her mouth, but nothing came out. She closed it again and nodded. 'I suppose. So,' she continued after a moment, 'I guess I should go to bed. Alone,' she said on an exhalation of breath that was as much disappointment as air.

He laughed. 'Or you could stay here and we could put the angel on the tree. And then,' he said, taking her hand, 'we could kiss some more.'

'But I thought you said—'

'Not going fast doesn't mean we can't stay in the same spot, Ava.'

He took the angel from the chair and put it on the top of the tree before pulling Ava back into his arms.

* * *

It was fine. It would all be fine. Fine. *Fine*. All completely fine.

Ava groaned as she made her way down the path that led to Leela's parents' house. Their property was gorgeous: beautiful green hills, tall trees and an incredible view of the Helderberg Mountain. And that didn't even include the view of the house: the tall white building that looked more like a showpiece than somewhere people lived.

But she barely saw it with her mind whirling around the way it was. Because this was the first time she'd see Noah since they'd spent that entire night making out. It had been an immensely satisfying evening, the kind she hadn't experienced in ages. But they hadn't slept together, and now, with the benefit of hindsight, Ava took solace in that fact.

Though it didn't help her feel any less guilty. And she knew that seeing Noah now, a week later, would be strange.

Still, she kept telling herself that it was fine.

Noah had helped her clean her house of soot the day after their night of making out, when she'd been allowed back onto the estate, and that had been fine. Granted, there had been touches and kisses, and maybe a half an hour of making out before he'd left, but things had been *fine*. Just as her work week—which had been so busy she hadn't had time to talk with him—had been fine.

It was all fine. Fine, fine, *fine.*

Which is why you're acting like a complete fool right now.

Ava paused, blew out a breath. And then inhaled deeply and exhaled for the same length of time. She was freaking out because of Noah, yes. But she knew it was also because this was the first wedding event where she'd have to face *people.* People who'd seen her fiancé walk away from her at her own wedding. People who'd seen the shock and hurt on her face.

She couldn't be surly. It would only prove to them that she'd had as hard a time about it as they believed. Besides, the time to be surly was over. It had been fine when they'd been planning. But now, with the rehearsal dinner, Leela and Jaden were actually starting their journey to committing to one another. She couldn't be surly about that.

And, in truth, she wasn't surly about *them.* She *wanted* Jaden and Leela to marry. She wanted them to be excited about their future together. She just hoped that neither of them would ever find out how it felt when all of it came crashing down around them.

Yeah, you're going to be completely fine.

Grunting at the stubborn voice in her heard, she squared her shoulders and walked into the house. It was beautifully decorated. Tables were decked with the wedding colours—blue and yellow—though not overly so, so that it looked like as much of a wedding celebration as a festive one. There was a Christmas tree in the corner; lights draped across the room. The sliding doors were open to the pool with the mountain view just beyond it.

Even Ava had to admit she was impressed.

'Are you ready?'

The voice sent a thrill down her spine, and gave her the opportunity to school her face before turning to face its owner.

'For what?'

Noah's eyes swept over her—she felt almost naked when she saw the greed there—but he only smiled. 'To lose.'

'To— Ha!' she said, though her heart was still thumping. 'Try again, Giles. I'm already leading in this game.'

'By twenty points. Don't think that's a head start you'll be able to keep.'

'I'm not worried. You're much too nice for your own good.'

His lips curved, and then he leaned over and brushed a kiss on her cheek. 'You look amazing.'

Again, his eyes swept over her. This time he kept the perusal slow, steady, as if he were actually undressing her. She shifted her weight between her feet, resisting the urge to brush a hand against the blue-and-white polka dot dress she'd worn for the event.

She'd made an effort with her looks—she'd even put a yellow ribbon in her hair, for heaven's sake—because she'd known that good behaviour wasn't a guarantee. The dress was long, but the neck plunged between her breasts, and she hadn't been able to wear a bra.

She regretted it immensely.

'I appreciate your compliments, but if you don't pull yourself together people are going to ask if we need a room.'

'Not a bad idea.'

'What isn't?'

Jaden joined them with a frown, and both she and Noah straightened.

'Doing my speech for Ava later tonight,' Noah said easily. 'So she can give me some pointers.'

Ava kept her eyes on Jaden, but she could feel her face warming. Noah's words had sounded dirtier than he'd intended. Or perhaps *as* dirty as he'd intended. She couldn't tell with him.

'I'm not sure that's a good idea,' Jaden replied, and Ava let out her breath. 'Ava's not the best public speaker.'

'Well, had I known that's what you think about me I wouldn't have agreed to this stupid slideshow.' Ava tilted her head. 'But now that I know what you think about me I suppose it gives me a certain freedom. Maybe I should talk about that holiday in Zanzibar when you—'

'Ava,' Jaden said with a wince. 'Would you please not talk about my past relationships at the rehearsal dinner of my wedding?'

'But it's part of the fun,' she teased.

'Just wait until you—' Jaden's eyes widened as he realised what he was about to say. 'Ava, I'm sorry. I didn't mean—'

'Oh, look, it's Uncle Cyril,' she interrupted him brightly. 'I think I'm going to talk to him about our cousins.'

She left before Jaden could apologise again. Before she could see more sympathy in his eyes.

CHAPTER THIRTEEN

'SHE'S JUST SAID she's going to talk to our uncle about the children he's estranged from.' Jaden groaned. 'Barely ten minutes in and I've already freaked her out.'

'I think that happened a long time ago,' Noah commented quietly, watching as Ava greeted the older man and began talking. He watched as the man put a hand on Ava's shoulder, saw her face blanch before she forced a smile and then said something that made the man frown.

She was playing the game by herself, he thought with a smile, and tried to figure out how he could make his way over to her without arousing suspicion.

'I don't know if that's true,' Jaden said, watching Ava, too.

Which, Noah thought in hindsight, was probably a good thing. He didn't know if his face held any of the lust—or those other pesky emotions—their kissing had brought to the surface.

'She hadn't been herself long before my wedding came along.'

'Really? Or is that just what you're telling yourself so you feel better about doing this at *this* time of year? Not to mention asking her to be in your wedding party after what happened?'

Jaden turned to him, his eyes narrowed. 'When did you become my sister's defender?'

'Since you've seemed to have abdicated the position.' As anger lit inside him Noah took a deep breath. 'But you can't even answer my questions, Jaden, which makes me think you *know* how hard this has been for her. And don't even try arguing with me. You know I'm right.'

Jaden lifted the side of his mouth, though it wasn't in a smile. 'I don't like it that you're taking her side over mine.'

'Man, are you *listening* to yourself?' Noah grabbed a glass of champagne from a waiter to distract himself from the annoyance that had taken his anger's place. 'This isn't about sides. This is about you supporting your little sister through a tough time.'

Jaden blew out a breath and then stole Noah's champagne, downing it before Noah could complain.

'Wait,' Jaden said. 'How do you even know about all this? How do you know this is tough for her?'

'She…er…she told me.'

'She *told* you?' Jaden repeated.

Realising he was losing the higher ground, Noah ran a hand over his hair. 'Yeah, but only because we were talking about the wedding after the fire on Friday—' He stopped too late.

'Exactly *when* after the fire did you speak with my sister?'

'Round about the same time she told me about Tiff being a bridesmaid.' He wasn't proud of it, but his ex had walked in and given him the perfect opportunity to regain control.

'Look, about that—'

'It's fine,' he interrupted when his guilt immediately flared. 'I mean, what could you have done? She introduced you to the woman you're going to spend your life with. Ava,' he answered Jaden's unspoken question.

'She really ran her mouth off with you,' Jaden said with a frown. Then he shook his head. 'I should have told you.'

'Yeah, you should have.'

'I'm sorry.' He paused. 'I've been caught up with this wedding. Maybe too caught up, since

I've been ignoring what Ava needs from me.' He set his empty champagne glass on a passing waiter's tray, and then patted Noah's back. 'But that doesn't mean you have free rein with my sister.'

'Wh—' Noah stopped, wondering how the conversation had turned pear-shaped again.

And because he didn't understand how—and because Jaden seemed to be in a strange mood and so did he—he didn't say what he wanted. That Ava wasn't an inanimate object. That she was a person with feelings. With agency.

'I don't know what you're talking about.'

'Yeah, you do.' Jaden said it easily, but there was a warning in his eyes. 'You know now and you knew it seven years ago, when you kissed her. She deserves more than what you've given the women who've come after Tiff.'

Jaden slapped him on the back again and walked away. It took Noah a few moments before he could figure out what had happened, and another few to process how he felt about what his best friend seemed to think of him.

But Jaden was right. Hadn't Noah himself thought about the control he exercised in his dating life not too long ago? The relationships he'd had after Tiff couldn't even be defined as such. There had been no emotions involved, on either side, and so no potential for hurt.

Still, Jaden's reaction had stung. More so because it was fair. And because now, after his conversation with Ava about his father—his mother—Noah knew his stance on relationships was more complicated than simply not wanting to repeat his father's mistakes.

He didn't want to repeat his father's pain.

He'd known it since the day Ava had told him about his father's advice to her to move on. But the more Noah thought about it, the more he'd realised that Kirk hadn't chosen to move on by forgetting about his wife's cheating, like Ava had said. No, Noah had been right when he'd thought his father was running.

But had he really thought that made his father weak? Because, if so, Noah was weak, too. Because though he'd chosen a different way to deal with it than his father had—choosing few to no relationships over a constant flow of them—Noah's motivations were the same. Except he didn't think he'd ever outrun the pain. His father's or his own.

It turned his stomach. And strengthened his resolve that he couldn't fall for Ava. Not any more than he already had. Not when he didn't know if his pain would allow him to give Ava what she needed.

Jaden was right: Ava deserved more than what Noah could give her. Especially while he figured out what exactly that was. But when his eyes settled on her, Noah felt everything inside him yearn. And he knew his resolve wouldn't be easy to follow.

'If it wasn't against the rules I'd deduct all your measly forty points for leaving me alone for half an hour. *Half an hour!*'

'I'm sorry.'

'You sound sincere, but I can't help but think that you did it on purpose. So that you wouldn't have to reward me handsomely for all my efforts.'

'That bad?'

Ava took a glass of champagne from a waiter and gave him a look. 'It's bad enough that I'm going to drink this glass of champagne instead of the sparkling water I'd intended on drinking tonight.'

She downed it and reached for another.

Noah put a hand on her free hand when she moved the glass to her lips again, and there was understanding in his eyes when he said, 'You don't want to get drunk tonight, Avalanche. You want to be here for your brother and future sister-in-law. You want to give a funny, yet charmingly embarrassing speech with your slideshow for all these guests. And then you want to go home and pretend it didn't happen.'

She gritted her teeth. Forced herself to relax when he squeezed her hand. And then told herself not to cry.

'This is…harder than I thought it was going to be.' She sipped from the champagne to hide the tears prickling in her eyes.

'I'm sorry.'

'Don't be.' She forced a smile. 'It's not your fault.'

'No. But maybe if I'd stayed you wouldn't be going through this.'

She gave him an even look, ignoring the thrill going up and down her spine. 'If you'd stayed, Noah, I think I would have been in a lot more trouble than I am now.'

Her eyes shifted to behind him, and something tightened inside her when she saw her parents. And then she saw Noah's father just behind them, and that something loosened slightly.

'Ava?' Noah said when she pulled her hand from his.

She nodded her head in the direction of the new guests, and felt him straighten beside her.

'Aunty Ruth… Uncle Sam,' Noah said, giving them both hugs before doing the same with his father.

It was so familiar that it sent a pang through her for all the years they'd missed. But, putting it aside, she kissed her parents and hugged Noah's father. Kirk gave her an extra pat on the back, signalling his support, and she smiled with a slight nod.

She hadn't had to tell Kirk how being in Jaden's wedding had made her feel. But when she'd made her way to Kirk's house after Leela had asked her to be a bridesmaid—eyes dry and heart aching—he'd patted her on the back just as he had now. And then he'd told her some innocuous story about work and she'd listened, refusing to think about real life for the rest of the day.

Somehow Kirk had known that being in the wedding would bring all the memories back. The memories of inadequacy. Of disgrace. Of failure. Somehow Kirk had known, and not even her own family had. But then, Kirk's experiences put him in a unique position to understand. And, since her family hadn't had those experiences, how could they know unless she'd told them?

You told Noah.

But Noah didn't know all of it. There was both a comfort and a despair in that.

Because she couldn't reconcile it, she sipped her champagne and chatted with her parents. And ignored the concerned looks both Noah and Kirk sent her.

Tonight wouldn't be one of those moments when she gave up her control. No matter how stressed she was, she would get through her slideshow. Even with her insides quivering at the weight of keeping it together, she would get through it.

She *would.*

Ava was suffering. It was in the slight shake of her hand when she brought the champagne flute to her lips. In the way she smiled at her parents but her eyes remained cautious. How the corners of her eyes were crinkled with strain. How her lips thinned whenever she wasn't fake smiling.

He didn't understand how the others couldn't see it. Or, if they could, how they didn't care. And, since he'd specifically told Jaden about it, Noah had to believe his friend was *choos-*

ing not to care. It bothered him so much he didn't know what to do with the anger vibrating through his body.

When it was announced that Ava wanted to say something about the happy couple, he almost snorted. There was no *want* in this situation. She'd been forced to say something. And, as miserable as she was about all of it, the fact that she'd agreed reinforced that she was determined to make the rest of her family believe she was okay. And make them feel better about themselves as a result.

Even at the cost of her own happiness.

He positioned himself towards the front of the room, ready in case something happened, though he wasn't entirely sure what could happen. But he wanted to make sure Ava knew he was there for her. He hadn't been before, but he would be now.

He tried not to think about what that meant for his determination not to fall for her.

'Hello, ladies and gentlemen,' Ava said into the microphone they'd handed her. 'For those of you who don't know me, I'm Jaden's baby sister, Ava. And for those of you who *do* know me, you must be wondering why in the world

Jaden would allow me to say something at his rehearsal dinner.'

The crowd laughed as Jaden pulled a face, his expression then relaxing into an easy smile. Noah turned his attention back to Ava. To anyone who didn't know her she'd look poised and relaxed. To those who did she looked tense and unhappy.

Noah clenched his jaw.

'But I managed to convince him so that I could tell you all how wonderful it is that he's finally found the love of his life in Leela.' She paused and smiled at them, and it seemed almost genuine. 'Actually, I'm going to *show* you, because I've come prepared with pictures!'

Noah was caught by her as she spoke, as she laughed, as she made the crowd laugh. She was perfect as she told stories of the different phases Jaden had gone through—goth phase included—and alluded to the women who'd been a part of those phases.

When she said that Leela had never been a part of any phase the crowd sighed. When she said she'd never seen her brother happier the crowd applauded. And when she wished them both well and toasted them the crowd drank to the couple and cheered as Ava kissed them both.

And still he was caught only by her. By the strength she'd shown in getting through it. By the love and affection she'd shown to her brother. Even though it had killed her.

When she left the room immediately afterwards Noah followed, finding her sitting at the top of the steps that led to Leela's parents' tennis court, her head in her hands.

'Hey,' he said quietly, sitting beside her, though all he wanted to do was take her into his arms and comfort her.

'Hey.' Her voice was raspy, but when she lifted her head, there were no tears on her face.

'That was pretty good,' he said after a moment.

'Funny and charmingly embarrassing?'

He chuckled. 'Exactly.'

'Great. So you'll support me as I get really, *really* drunk now?'

'You don't want to do that.'

'I don't.' She sighed. 'I just want to stop hurting.'

CHAPTER FOURTEEN

THE WORDS SAT between them and Noah didn't know what to do with them. He didn't want to push, but he also didn't want her to ruminate on it.

Just ask, dummy.

Nearly rolling his eyes at his inner voice, he said, 'Do you want to talk about it?'

'I don't think anyone's ever asked me that,' she replied after a long moment. 'Everyone just assumes I *don't* want to talk about it. Which is fair. I don't. But nor do they.' She paused. 'The Kellers have a talent for pretending things didn't happen. Or hiding their feelings about it.'

'Can't say I've noticed,' he commented dryly.

She laughed. 'You're practically part of the family and yet it hasn't affected *you*.'

'I'm not sure that's true.'

'Isn't it?' she asked, but didn't wait for an answer. 'You've always seemed pretty self-aware to me.'

'I'm not. I've only just realised I've been

angry with my father for trying to protect himself from hurt. And that I've been blaming him for—' He broke off, knowing he couldn't say any more. Instead he picked up a stone and threw it across the court, wincing when it hit the net. 'I'm probably going to have to pick that up.'

'Probably.'

Silence lingered between them.

'I think…' He started to speak without realising, and when his mind caught up to his mouth he almost stopped. But then he thought that the words were already there, and that if he wanted *her* to talk he needed to talk, too. 'Maybe you think I'm self-aware because something about you makes me feel like I can share things with you.'

'Or maybe you just need to talk.'

'No, it's you.'

'That's not true.'

'It's definitely true. Why else would I be sitting outside with you after your brother warned me not to? I could—'

'Wait—what?' She frowned. 'My brother told you *not* to come outside and sit with me?'

'Your brother told me that I needed to stay away from you.' He shrugged, but his emotion didn't feel as careless as the gesture.

'What a—' She stopped, shook her head. 'He had no right to do that.'

'He's looking out for you.' He paused. 'I don't know why he's decided to do that now. When it's too late to keep you from hurting like this.'

'He can't protect me from life,' she said after a moment. 'I fell in love. Got my heart broken. And he was there for me all through it.'

'He should have sussed the guy out. Clearly he wasn't right for you.'

'You don't know that.'

'I *do* know that,' he said. 'You're here, in pain, and not with this man. He wasn't right for you. And I bet you knew that long before he left you at the altar.'

She didn't reply, and suddenly something occurred to him.

'I'm sorry. I'm crossing the line.' His heart ached as he said it. 'I just assumed—'

'What?'

'That you're over him. I shouldn't have said—'

'No.' She interrupted him quietly. 'I *am* over him.'

She took a deep breath and lifted a hand to her face, before clasping it with her other hand and lowering them both between her knees.

'I'm not over what he did to me, but I'm over

him.' She turned to look at him. 'You're right. He wasn't the right man.'

When unspoken words—unspoken emotions—stirred the air between them, hijacking the silence, highlighting the tension, Noah cleared his throat.

'So why didn't Jaden *do* something? Why didn't he warn the guy like he did me?'

'Maybe his warning abilities only came after his engagement.'

He laughed. 'Oh, no, those abilities have been alive and well since that time he caught us kissing. I still remember our discussion.' He winced. 'That's probably too civil a word, but you get the idea.'

He felt her surprise before he saw it. Before she angled her body; before her features twisted into an expression he'd have thought cute if he hadn't seen her eyes. If he hadn't seen the confusion, the anger, the hurt there.

The hurt bothered him the most.

'Exactly what kind of discussion, if not civil?'

'I…er…we just spoke about how inappropriate my actions were.'

'Your actions?' she repeated, tilting her head as she shifted even further away from him.

'You mean when you kissed yourself? Or when you kissed me and there was no reciprocation?'

'Ava, it's not—'

'Because *your* actions were inappropriate that day?' She stood now. 'Me wrapping my legs around you, pressing my body against yours, asking you—both verbally and non-verbally— to take me back to your place and—'

'Ava, please.' He stood now, too, his legs shaky. He couldn't hear her say those words again. Not when he'd been successfully running from them for most of the last seven years. 'You're upset about everything that's happened today—'

'How would *you* know?' She put her hands on her hips. '*What* do you know other than what I've told you?'

'Ava—'

'*No*, Noah. I can't be the bigger person right now. I can't pretend you blocking my emails doesn't bother me. Or ignore the fact that you've talked about me with my brother like I'm some kind of possession and not a woman with the ability to make my own decisions. Or,' she said with a frown, 'how that talking with my brother probably *led* to you blocking me.'

He gave a curt nod—he was helpless not to

when she'd just confirmed everything he'd already known—and she rolled her eyes.

'Why the hell do I even bother?' she asked.

And walked away.

Men were ridiculous. They were annoying. They were the *worst*.

If she had her way she'd never have to deal with them again. Or at the very least she wouldn't have to stay at a dinner during which she was forced to look into the faces of two men who reminded her how ridiculous—annoying, the *worst*—they really were.

She'd detoured the moment she'd re-entered the room after her chat with Noah and had seen Jaden heading for her. Had gone so far as to wait in the bathroom for twenty minutes—not fun—so that she wouldn't have to speak with him.

By the time she came out the dinner was starting and Jaden was preoccupied. Noah, on the other hand, seemed to have been waiting for her. He nodded his head to the empty seat next to him and she nearly laughed. He thought she was going to sit next to *him*? Maybe she *should* have laughed, just to show him how ridiculous he was being.

Instead she ignored him and took a seat next to her parents.

How she got through the rest of the stupid evening, she had no idea. But as soon as dinner had ended and she knew people would no longer care whether she was there or not, she tried to leave the party.

Tried.

'Ava—wait.'

Ava clenched her jaw, then relaxed it and turned to face her aunt. She'd been avoiding the woman since she'd seen her glide in as if she was the queen of the party. Taking in her jewels and overly formal dress, Ava thought her aunt might actually believe that she was.

'I've been trying to speak with you all evening.'

'Really?' Ava arranged an easy smile on her face. 'I didn't realise.'

'I wanted to know how you've been.'

'Just peachy. I mean, as peachy as I *can* be after my fiancé—whom I loved—left me at the altar in front of my friends and family.'

Her aunt blinked, and satisfaction rippled through Ava. This was what her aunt wanted, wasn't it? To revel in Ava's misery. To take pleasure from the fact that her niece was struggling.

'Yes, well, that *was* what I wanted to know.' Her aunt smiled sympathetically. 'I can't imagine what it's like to rebuild your life after something like that happens.'

'Hard. I've had days when I didn't want to get out of bed. Nights when I couldn't stop thinking about what was wrong with me. And then, of course, there are the people. Those who—for some strange reason—want to know about *what* happened without really caring *who* it happened to.' She let out a little sigh. 'Honestly, celebrating another wedding this soon has made *everything* better.'

There was a beat between Ava's last word and the feeling of utter dread as she realised she'd taken it too far. Damn it, why did she always take it too far?

'You told me you weren't going to keep on pulling people's legs like this, Ava!'

Ava's spine stiffened at Noah's voice, before her mind processed his words.

'I can't help it.' She gave him a smile she hoped was teasing, but she honestly couldn't be sure. 'It's so easy.'

'I know. But you make them panic.' Noah handed her a glass of champagne that he took from a waitress nearby and smiled at Ava's aunt. 'It was a running joke between us until I realised that she was freaking out her family.'

'This…this is a *joke*?'

'Afraid so.' Noah's smile was effortlessly charming. 'You know Ava's sense of humour.'

'I—I don't think I do.'

If Ava hadn't already embarrassed herself, she would have enjoyed her usually self-assured aunt's stammering.

'Of *course* you do,' Noah said, his smile widening. 'It's from her mother's side of the family.'

Ava stifled her laugh, and there was a long pause before her aunt gave a polite excuse and walked away.

It was just the two of them then, and she handed him back the champagne flute.

'Seventy points. It would be higher, but you used my embarrassment to get your points.'

'Which, in my humble opinion, should be the reason I get at least ninety points. I saw an opportunity and I went for it.'

'Eighty. That's my final offer.'

She didn't wait to see if he accepted, instead turning to the front door so that she could leave as she'd wanted to in the first place.

She got as far as the steps that led to the pathway a few metres from the door.

'You don't want to know how many points I gave you?'

She turned. 'For embarrassing myself?'

'For embarrassing your aunt. The point of this game.'

'Fine,' she said after a beat. 'How many?'

'Twenty.'

'Twenty?' She rolled her eyes. 'Keep your points.'

'Well, you started with fifty, by calling your aunt out for asking about you but not really caring. Then you lost thirty for lying about how you feel. Ten for each lie.'

'I didn't lie.'

'You said that you've struggled to get out of bed—' he lifted a finger '—that you've wondered what was wrong with you—' another finger '—and that you *want* to be in this wedding.' He lifted a third.

Tired now, she sighed. 'You only have to deduct ten points. There was only one lie.'

She walked down the stairs and didn't bother to look back or stop when he called to her.

CHAPTER FIFTEEN

HE COULDN'T LET her leave like that. Not when he knew which one the lie was. Not when, after the second time she'd told him something was wrong with her, the truth made his stomach turn.

He ran until he was next to her, and when she sighed he ignored it.

'Just leave me alone.'

'Not when you're in this mood.'

She grunted, but again he ignored it. Instead he kept walking beside her, as if somehow his presence would manage to convince her that she could talk to him. That she could trust him.

But by the time they reached the car park, she still hadn't said anything.

He considered what he'd do if she got into her car and left the party. Would he get into his and follow her? He hadn't said goodbye to anyone—not Jaden, not his father—but he supposed he could make something up to satisfy them. But then he remembered the look Jaden had given him earlier—when he'd returned to the party shortly after Ava had—and he wondered whether anything he made up would be believable.

In the end he didn't have to make the decision. Ava stalked past her car and took a path just beyond the car park that he hadn't seen before. He hung back when the path became too narrow for him to walk next to her, and although he wanted to ask where they were going he just looked around him.

The path was enclosed by vines that created an archway the entire way down. Soft pink flowers clung to the vines and, without thinking, he picked one, then awkwardly stared at it in his hand. Before he could decide what to do with it his attention was drawn to the fact that the path had ended, opening up to a medium-sized dam hidden from the main property.

'Have you been here before?' he asked in a breathless voice, too amazed that something like this could actually be on someone's property to care.

'Once. A long time ago.'

She kicked off her shoes, tossed her bag to the side, then pulled her dress up to expose her legs to mid-thigh.

'It was during the day, at an extravagant

party much like the one at the house now.' She breathed in deeply, and as she exhaled she looked at the sky. 'Personally, I prefer it like this. With the stars reflecting in the water from the sky. And a small ball of silver right over there for the moon.'

She nodded her head in its direction, and then walked to the edge of the dam, the water lapping over her feet.

'I don't know if that's a good idea, Ava,' he said carefully, as memories of the two of them in a similar situation taunted him.

'I don't care if it's a good idea.' She'd walked deeper into the water now, and it reached to her knees. 'It's cool and refreshing and it's making me feel better so I don't care.'

After a few more minutes he realised he wasn't going to convince her to sit on the grass with him. Sighing, he kicked off his own shoes, removed his socks and rolled up his black trousers.

He put his phone and wallet on top of the rest of their belongings and walked to the water. He hissed when the water touched his feet. But when she looked over lazily, and he was drawn by the seduction of it, he no longer cared that *cool and refreshing* wasn't quite how he'd describe the water.

'What are you doing, Noah?'

Even her words were seductive, he thought. But he didn't know if she'd intended them to be. Which made it even worse.

'You need someone to talk to,' he answered, instead of saying what he wanted to say. *I need to get you out of that dress and into my arms.* 'I'm here.'

She arched an eyebrow and his heart kicked.

'Something tells me that's not the only thing you're here for.'

Of *course* she'd be able to see through him.

'It's the only thing I'm asking for.'

Their eyes held for a moment, and then she shook her head. 'Why is it so important to you that I talk?'

'Because you've kept it all in for too long.' He paused. 'And you haven't told anyone what you're really feeling.'

'How do you know that?'

'I spoke with Jaden earlier. His reaction made me think that you haven't told *him* what you're feeling. The fact that your parents aren't rallying around makes me believe that you haven't told them either. And the way my father kept checking on you tonight tells me he suspects something, but doesn't know. And then, of course, there's the fact that you're standing here, almost waist-deep in a dam, which makes me think there are things you haven't figured out. Probably because you haven't said them out loud.'

She blew out a breath, and when her eyes met his they glistened slightly.

He took a step forward, but she shook her head, and he stopped. And then she sighed.

'Well, Noah, you're not wrong. Though I wish you were.'

Ava drew her dress up higher, so that the material of its skirt bunched just below her breasts. Then she moved deeper into the water.

'I wish it were as simple as this wedding reminding me of the one I didn't have,' she continued. 'Or a Christmas wedding being a special reminder of my failure.'

'You didn't fail.'

'Of course I did.'

She spun, enjoying the way it sent ripples out across the rest of the water. Enjoying how it seemed so simple, uncomplicated. It inspired her to get through the rest of the conversation in the same way, even if what she was talking about *wasn't* simple and uncomplicated.

'I loved Christmas,' she said, just twisting gently now. It kept the ripples going, but didn't threaten her dress. 'You know how much I loved it.'

'Based on your opinion of my house, I thought you still did.'

Her lips curved at the dryness in his tone. 'I guess I still have some of that love inside me. But most of it's gone.' She sighed. 'The festivities I used to love just feel contrived now. The family time feels forced. Complicated and heavy. The things I used to love feel like they were a lifetime ago. Putting the tree up. Drinking and eating and laughing.'

'*We* just did that.'

'We did,' she said, surprise fluttering through her. 'But it was easier with you. You didn't keep looking at me to check if I was okay.'

'No,' he agreed. 'My reasons were different.'

She laughed softly. 'You're flirting with me even now?'

'Is it flirting if I'm being earnest?'

Not knowing how to answer him, she continued with the rest of her story. 'You weren't here. You didn't have to see how I looked when Milo left me in front of everyone I knew and loved. You didn't have to see me put on a brave smile as I followed him down the aisle, running after him as soon as I got out of that church.'

She tightened her grip on her dress.

'You didn't have to see him drive away and me sink to the floor. You didn't have to see me stay there, unable to cry because I knew people were watching me. You didn't have to help me up. You didn't have to help me into a car. And you didn't have to see me curl into a ball on my way home.'

'Ava…' he whispered.

She heard the horror in his tone. But all desire for simplicity had gone out of the window now. She'd been captured by her own tale. Ensnared by the emotions. The memories.

'I think the worst thing for them was that I was determined not to show anyone he'd hurt me. Halfway to my house I uncurled from the ball and demanded we go back to the church. And then I marched back in and told everyone we had food and alcohol and the party would go on.'

She laughed at her audacity now, and the sound was harsh.

'I made sure I spoke with every single person who attended that reception. I explained to them that Milo and I had made a mistake and decided to go our separate ways. That I was fine and he was fine, and I assured them they could enjoy themselves. Even though I hadn't spoken to Milo I already knew we wouldn't get back together. He'd humiliated me. And he didn't have the decency to tell me why. He didn't deserve me.'

'He didn't,' Noah said fiercely. 'He didn't deserve you.'

'Except,' she said softly, almost as if he hadn't spoken at all, 'I couldn't believe that. Not entirely. I could only think that there must be something wrong with *me*. That *I* didn't deserve *him*.'

'He told you that when he eventually spoke with you, didn't he?'

'Not in so many words.' She took a breath. 'He came to my house the next day. I'd sent my family away because I needed time. I wanted to stop pretending. I didn't want to be "on", and with them I felt like I had to be.'

She paused.

'He said I was too much work.' She blinked, and felt wetness fall down her cheeks. 'As if I were a project that needed tackling. As if I were a dilapidated house that needed to be rebuilt.' She looked at Noah now. Noted the fierce look in his eyes. Heard it echo in her tone. 'We were together for five years, and on our wedding day he discovered that he didn't want to work on this *project*. This *house*.'

'Please tell me he's somewhere in the world missing a digit.'

She gave him a look, though his words steadied her. 'If I'd removed something from his body, it wouldn't have been a finger or toe.'

He grimaced, and then laughed. 'Fair point.' He walked to her now, apparently not noticing he was soaking his trousers in the process. 'You're not too much work.'

'I might be.' She swallowed, and stilled when he brushed a thumb across her cheek, spreading the wetness of her tears over her skin.

'Not too much. Just…work. We're all work.'

'Not all of us are left at the altar because of it.'

'Because some of us are too scared to take that chance.'

He frowned, and she realised he was talking about himself. Perhaps he'd just discovered it about himself, and was reassuring her about something he didn't really believe was true.

'Taking chances is overrated,' she said under her breath.

He laughed, breaking the tension. 'I doubt most people in the world would agree with you.'

'Most people in the world haven't been left at the altar,' she said again. 'I have the moral high ground here, Noah. You don't want to mess with—'

She stopped as a huge wave of water washed over her. Partly because she was surprised— they were in a dam; there were no waves—and partly because all her efforts to keep her dress dry were now in vain.

'Did you—' She wiped the water from her face. 'Did you just *splash* me? When my hair and face are *perfectly* made up? When my dress—which is *very* expensive—is still—'

She was silenced by another wave of water. This time she didn't bother coming up. Instead, she sank under the water, knowing that inevitable panic would cause Noah to come closer.

Just as she'd thought, she felt his leg against her belly, and before he could do anything she'd come up in front of him and was pulling him down with her.

A part of her knew that he was letting her drag him down. He was much too strong for just the weight of her arms to pull him under. But, as if he'd accepted his punishment, he stayed under the water for as long as she held him down.

When they came up, he flicked his hair back and wiped his face.

'Fair.'

She stared, and then laughed. 'Of *course* that's all you're saying about this.'

He lifted a shoulder. 'It *is* fair. I started it.'

'Why?'

'It seemed like the perfect way to distract you.'

Softening, she rolled her eyes. 'Yeah, well, it's not only going to distract me, but also the entire party when we go back up there in soaked clothing.'

He winced. 'I didn't think about that.'

'No, I didn't think you did.' She sighed and pushed herself deeper into the water. 'But we're here now, and we're probably going to get into trouble anyway, so we might as well enjoy it.'

He hadn't thought his actions through, but now, watching Ava relax in the water, he couldn't make himself regret it.

'What is it with you and water?' he asked suddenly, surprising himself. 'You've always been at your happiest when you're swimming.'

'I don't know,' she said, straightening where she'd been floating on her back. 'I guess it was all the family holidays we spent in the water. Beaches, swimming pools, dams...' She sighed happily. 'Good memories.'

'I agree.'

Her eyes met his and immediately the energy around them snapped. He could have sworn he saw the water boiling. Because, as he'd intended, his words had made her think about the last time they'd been in the water together. About the memories they'd created then.

'No,' she breathed when he closed the distance between them.

Dutifully, he stopped. 'I'm sorry.'

'Don't be. I just... You mess with my head. And kissing you...' She shook her head.

And even though the curls on her head were misshapen with water—even though the make-up on her face was smudged—she was still the most beautiful woman he'd ever been drawn to.

'You don't think that's true for me, too? Because I guarantee what happened last week has kept me awake *every single night* since then. Fortunately, I'm only going back to the station after the wedding.'

'And you can take photos without having slept?'

'I can,' he confirmed, 'but I don't have to. I work freelance. According to my own terms. According to my own time. I've given myself some time off.'

She sucked her lip between her teeth and his body tightened.

'This isn't a good idea,' she said, but she swam closer and lifted her dress under the water, wrapping her legs around his waist.

'I know.' He put his hands under her butt and brought her tight against his body, so her mouth hovered just above his.

'Jaden could find us.'

'I don't care.'

'What about the warning?'

'I'm going to hell anyway, Ava. Might as well go down swinging.'

And with those words he kissed her.

No matter how many times he'd kissed her, it always felt new. Different. And yet somehow there was a familiarity that made every movement of their lips seductive.

The other times, he'd taken his time kissing her. Kissing was a leisure activity, after all. Created to be savoured, enjoyed. And kissing Ava had strengthened that belief for him. Her tongue moved in intuitive ways, and sent shimmers of pleasure through him. Her lips were soft, inviting, and pressed against his as if they belonged there.

Kissing her leisurely gave him the opportunity to feel the softness of her body under his hands. To feel its contrast with the hardness of his own. To enjoy the curves of her, the lines of her. To have desire travel lazily through him. To have awareness torture him.

Which was why it made no sense that he was kissing her now as if there would never be any more kisses.

He could sense her surprise as he deepened their kiss. But there was no resistance, and she tightened her arms around his neck, angling her mouth and inviting him to take more.

So he did.

He took and took, and wasn't surprised when she demanded more from him, too. Because that was who Ava was. Power. Fire. Strength. She matched him with every stroke; returned every caress with equal passion.

His fingers—his body—wanted more, and he suspected hers did, too. Just as he suspected that they would have both taken more—given more—if they hadn't been interrupted.

CHAPTER SIXTEEN

SHE NEEDED TO STOP. To stop kissing Noah. To stop kissing him in water. To stop enjoying the feel of his body under her fingers. But most of all she needed to stop kissing Noah in water, feeling his body under her fingers and *getting caught*.

As soon as she heard the giggling she pushed away from him. And then, for good measure, swam a short distance out. She rolled her eyes at herself, knowing that no one who stumbled upon them was going to believe that they were just there to talk. Even if that *had* been what they'd been doing initially.

But if she'd thought being caught kissing her brother's best friend was awkward, she wasn't prepared for the awkwardness of being caught by her brother's best friend's *father*…and the woman he was clearly sneaking off to make out with.

If the water around them had heated when they'd started kissing, it had iced over now.

Noah's face had gone completely blank, though there was a twitch at his eye that betrayed his feelings.

'Noah,' Kirk said, his hand firm on the small of his guest's back.

Ava didn't recognise the woman, so she assumed it was one of Leela's friends. If she didn't hate being in this situation—seeing what it did to Noah—she would have been amused.

'I didn't realise anyone was here.'

Noah didn't reply. He just walked out of the water, and turned to Ava, his hand outstretched. She immediately started towards him—trying not to think about how her dress clung her body, or the fact that it was even more incriminating that she wasn't wearing a bra—and took his hand as soon as she could.

'We'll leave you two alone,' Noah said as they walked over and picked up their things.

'Noah—'

'It's fine,' Noah interrupted his father, giving him a smile that looked more like a grimace. 'I'll see you at lunch tomorrow.'

Her hand still caught in Noah's, she gave Kirk an apologetic look before following Noah to the car park. The journey was short, but the heaviness in the air around them made it feel endless, as if they were still moving through water.

She gave a sigh of relief once they got to the car park and saw that most of the cars were still there. Since she had her keys with her, she could leave without showing anyone what a mess she was. Or facing the inevitable questions when they saw who she'd got into a mess with.

'Are you okay?' she asked quietly, when Noah didn't take any steps towards his car.

'Fine.'

She winced. 'You don't have to pretend to be fine.'

'No?' When he turned to her, his eyes were cold. 'So you want to know what's going on inside my head after seeing my father sneaking off to—' He broke off on a curse.

'Yes. If it's going to make you feel better then, yes, tell me.'

'It won't make me feel better,' he said flatly. 'It's just going to annoy me even more.'

He walked towards his car then, but she hurried forward, blocking his path.

'Tell me.'

He didn't reply. Only moved to walk around her.

She shifted again. 'Tell me, Noah.'

'Nothing good will come out of it if I do, Ava,' he said in a warning tone. 'Just let me go.'

'I've confided in you—' she swallowed when the words caused her stomach to churn '—because I trust you. You can trust me, too.'

'And how is trusting you going to change the fact that seeing my father back there just reminded me that I can't run from my family's past?' he asked tightly. 'That no matter how much I want to, *I can't run*?'

The despair in his voice was the reason Ava didn't stop him when he walked past her this time. A few minutes later, he drove away. It happened so quickly that she was still staring at the dust his car had left behind long after it was gone.

And then, when she heard voices, she hurried to her own car and left, too.

It was late that night before she allowed herself to think about it. It was a coping mechanism she'd developed that was conducive to productivity but a nightmare for sleep. She could do everything she needed to do and ignore her thoughts, her emotions, but the minute she got into bed she'd think about it all.

It meant that she'd got a lot done after the end of her engagement. It also meant that she'd had too little sleep to be able to function in those first few months. She'd been on leave at first—had gone on her honeymoon alone, forced herself to enjoy it, or at least pretend to—and had returned more tired than when she'd gone an entire year without a single break.

She'd tried to keep doing her job, but the words had swum in front of her face, and the copy she'd turned in had been so riddled with errors her manager had suggested she take the rest of her leave days to try and pull herself together.

It had hurt her pride, that request. It had also caused her to realise the pride she'd thought she'd lost after being jilted was still there, alive and kicking. It had spurred her to the animal shelter the next day, and prompted her to ask for their least sought-after cat.

When they'd shown her Zorro—and told her how he'd been abused as a kitten—she'd fallen in love immediately. He was the ugliest cat she'd ever seen, but when he'd rested his steady gaze on her she'd seen something there she didn't think anyone else had. Feeling a pull to that—feeling it resonate within herself—she'd adopted him.

And from the moment she'd brought Zorro

home she'd felt better. She'd been able to go back to work the next week, and had worked her butt off to make sure her team knew she wouldn't be making the same mistakes.

It hadn't mattered that she'd still cried at night sometimes. It hadn't mattered that there had still been days when she'd felt as if she were a collection of puzzle pieces unable to fit together again. The only thing that had mattered was that the world saw her as whole. And if the world thought she was, maybe she'd believe it, too.

It had worked for the most part. Until this stupid wedding had come along—until it had brought Noah back and she had been forced to face just how incomplete she was. She didn't need the added complication of falling for Noah. Of being reminded of her feelings for him. Or that once upon a time she'd dreamt about a wedding for the two of them.

He'd hurt her when he'd left all those years ago. And, like most things in her life, she'd avoided thinking about it until she no longer could. Because she knew that if she acknowledged that Noah had hurt her she would have to acknowledge other things, too. That she'd put herself out there to *be* hurt. Because she'd had feelings for him.

And, as annoyed as she'd been at Noah for entertaining her brother's protectiveness back then, she knew that Jaden's feelings had affected the way she'd felt about the situation, too. She hadn't been able to imagine unsettling their relationship for something that would go nowhere. And, based on the way both she and Noah had responded to one another seven years ago, she hadn't seen it going anywhere.

But she could now. And the events of that night—his support, their arguments, the revelations, the kissing—told her she was right. Except that she wasn't sure she *wanted* it to go anywhere. Because if she did she'd have to face her very real fear: that she didn't deserve him.

Noah had known the lunch with his father was going to be awkward and long before he'd seen his father giggling with a woman half his age. But not that long before, he thought. In fact, the exact moment had been when his father had caught his eye as he'd been trying to get Ava's attention during the rehearsal dinner. Kirk had just raised a brow at him, but it had been enough.

So Noah wasn't too surprised at the silence that reigned during most of their lunch.

'Are you looking forward to the wedding?' his father asked, after their waiter had brought their starters and their conversation still hadn't consisted of much other than 'hello'.

'For Jaden's sake, yes.'

'But not for your own?'

He forked a crumbed mushroom with more force than necessary. 'Do people *ever* look forward to other people's weddings for their own sake?'

His father didn't reply, and Noah realised that was why silence was better. Everything was a minefield. An innocuous question about the wedding could lead down a very dark path. Noah had almost asked his father if *he* was looking forward to the wedding for his own sake. It *was* a decent place to pick up women, after all.

He popped another mushroom into his mouth and forced himself to chew. He didn't like the tone of the voice in his head. It sounded just like the part of him that still blamed his father, though he knew it wasn't fair.

'Ava tells me the two of you have struck up a friendship since I've been gone,' he said.

Oh, yes, because that *question won't explode in your face.*

'Yes.' Kirk's face softened. 'She's sweet. Didn't deserve the mess of last year.'

His father picked up his beer and took a long drag from it before shaking his head.

'I'll never forget the look on her face when that man walked out—'

'You were there?'

'Yes.' Kirk frowned. 'I thought you knew that?'

'I didn't realise your friendship had secured you an invitation to the wedding.'

'I was more her parents' guest than hers,' Kirk told him. 'We're friends, just like you and Jaden are. Though I think Ava was happy I was there.'

He chose not to reply to that, his mood too dark for him to trust what he might have said. Instead, he took a deep breath. And then he asked, 'Why didn't you tell me Ava was getting married?'

'Would you have wanted to know?'

'What kind of a question is *that*?'

'The kind a father asks when he knows that his son ignored his own invitation to said wedding.'

'That wasn't because I didn't want to know.' Noah clenched his jaw. 'I didn't get it.'

'Why not?'

'I—' He took a sip of water. 'I blocked her email address.'

'Why?'

'Because—' He shook his head. 'It's complicated.'

'Well, you'd better *un*complicate it, son. Ava's been through enough without you messing with her head.'

Noah stared at his father. 'You know *I'm* your son, right? You're not supposed to choose a random woman—' He broke off with a hiss. 'I'm sorry. I didn't mean that.'

'You probably did. And we'll get to that.' Kirk ate some of his salad before continuing. 'But in terms of Ava... You and I both know she's not "a random woman".'

Chastised—and more than a little jolted by his father's perceptiveness—he nodded.

'And I don't agree that my warning you against messing with her is choosing her over you. Especially since something tells me you're probably messed up about this, too.' He paused. 'So, if your plans don't involve you staying here long enough to clean up any mess you've made, you shouldn't be out swimming with her at midnight.'

He couldn't argue with that. Besides, Kirk had just given Noah the perfect segue into telling him why he'd arranged this lunch in the first place.

'I'll be here,' he said slowly. 'I'm moving back home.'

His father blinked. 'Back home?'

'Yeah.' He rubbed a hand over the back of his neck. 'I'm taking a break from photography for a while. At least, unofficially.'

'Are you moving back or are you taking a break?' His father's voice was stern. 'Those are two different things.'

They were, but he was trying to find a diplomatic way of telling his father about his plans. Now he thought being honest might be easier.

'I'm moving back, Dad. Permanently. And I'm taking a break from photography while I figure out what I want to do while I'm here.'

His father nodded slowly. 'Why?' he asked after a moment.

'I've missed you.'

Kirk reached out and squeezed Noah's hand. 'I've missed you, too. And you know I'd love to have you home again. But you left for a reason. What's changed?'

'Me.' He'd answered without thinking and now he realised it was the truth. 'And—I hope—us.'

Kirk stared at him for a moment, and then nodded. 'Let's start with us.' He paused. 'How about you tell me why seeing me with that woman last night upset you?'

CHAPTER SEVENTEEN

'TORTURE,' AVA SAID, unashamed of how miserable she sounded. 'It's bad enough that I have to do all this wedding stuff at Christmas, but now there are unexpected little meetings like this? To do what? Fold boxes for Christmas cookies? You're torturing me, Jaden.'

Jaden grimaced. 'If I had a choice, none of us would be folding any boxes.' He paused. 'I *am* sorry that this is at Christmas, though.'

She sighed. 'No, you're just sorry that it's *this* Christmas.'

She'd arrived at Jaden's house early, so that she could scold him privately for all the things Leela had been demanding in the last week. After all, she could hardly complain to the bride. But she knew that part of her motivation was also because she was still annoyed at him for his overprotectiveness of her with Noah.

Which she couldn't talk to him about directly. Because that was *not* a conversation she needed to have.

She walked to the fridge, looked longingly at the wine, but dismissed the thought instantly. She didn't need any more reason to loosen her tongue. Instead, she took out a soft drink can.

'Would it have been better at any other Christmas?'

Ava took a sip of her drink and turned to her brother. It was the first time they'd got anywhere close to discussing what had happened the year before. Or how his wedding might be affecting her.

'I think so. Time always makes things easier.'

Jaden nodded. 'You probably hate me for all this.'

'I don't hate you. I'm annoyed, yes. But not at you. At myself for...for the entire mess.'

She didn't pull away from him when he walked over and put an arm around her waist, resting her head on his shoulder instead.

'I didn't ever think it would go bad. Now, after everything, I'm annoyed that it was Christmas and that a holiday I used to love has been tainted in this way. And I... I blame myself for all of it.'

Jaden's face tightened, and he pulled her into a hug. She let herself be comforted by him—knowing it would be the only time she'd allow it—before she pulled away and took a step back.

'Now, let's just get through the box-folding and whatever other delights Leela has in store for us before the wedding, shall we?'

He smiled at her, but she thought she saw something on his face that looked almost reckless.

A moment later it was gone, and then the doorbell rang and Ava pushed it out of her head. It wouldn't benefit her, so what was the point in thinking about it? Besides, she had enough to think about now that she'd said something to Jaden about how she felt. And then there was Noah, whom she hadn't seen or spoken to since the rehearsal dinner the week before.

She greeted Leela and Tiff, who had arrived at the same time, but didn't move to hug her future sister-in-law as she should have because she had no desire to hug Tiff.

Not that she had anything against the woman. She just—

No, she did have something against the woman.

Tiff had had Noah's heart once. And she'd stomped on it. Ava was pretty sure that was part of what he'd alluded to last week. But she was a civil person—most days—and she could be an adult.

An adult who won't hug a woman because of her past with the man you—

If Ava had ever experienced stopping her thoughts in their tracks, it was in that moment, when that very annoying voice in her head was taking liberties with the truth. *Liberties.* Because the actual truth was too terrifying to consider.

It tested her commitment to civility, so that when Noah and Ken arrived she only nodded at them, and simmered in her anger as she watched Tiff hug Noah.

'Well, everyone, thank you for coming on such short notice,' Leela said once everyone was settled with a drink. 'I know we've been putting you through the wringer with this wedding, but we really appreciate your help and support. So tonight—'

'So tonight, as a thank-you,' Jaden interrupted, ignoring the surprise on Leela's face, 'we're going to be taking you all to the Christmas carnival at the high school down the road.'

Ava couldn't help the chuckle that left her lips at this announcement. Jaden shot her a look— *I'm doing this for you. Please don't get me into any more trouble*—and she turned it into a cough before gleefully clasping her hands together.

'This is the absolute *best* news you could have given us, Jaden!' she said.

Again with the acting, Ava thought. But this time it was for a much nobler cause than when she'd been lying for her cat. Or teasing Noah.

She was saving her brother's future marriage.

'I can't believe you and Leela thought of thanking us in such a considerate way. By taking us to the carnival you and I used to go to every year at Christmas!'

Now she stood to hug both Leela and Jaden. When she got to her brother, she whispered, 'Thank you,' and then stood back and did a quick jump. 'This is *wonderful*!'

Leela gave her an uneasy smile. 'You're welcome.'

'Tricking us into believing we needed to fold boxes,' Noah added, smirking when Ava looked at him and realised that Jaden had given *him* a look, too. 'You're sneaky, future Mr and Mrs Jaden Keller. But we love you anyway.'

'Yes, well,' Leela said, her smile fading somewhat. 'We should probably get to it, then.'

* * *

'On a scale of one to ten, what are the chances Leela is going to castrate Jaden tonight?'

'One,' Ava said immediately. 'She wants a big family. She wouldn't risk it. However, I can't say the same for his limbs.'

Noah chuckled, more from relief that she'd answered than from what she'd said. He hadn't heard from her all week, though he knew that was because they'd been busy. She was still working, and he'd been helping Jaden with the wedding, and editing some pictures he'd taken before he'd come back home.

But he wasn't sure that that was it. He hadn't spoken to her since he'd acted like an ass—and revealed why in his little outburst—the night of the rehearsal dinner. He'd told himself to call her, but that had required a courage he hadn't conjured up yet. He'd also spent a lot of his energy trying to process the conversation he'd had with his father that day at lunch.

All of which were, of course, excuses.

'I think you deserve some points for your acting back there.'

'You know, I'm not even going to argue that that's against the rules. I accept.'

'Firstly, of course you do. Secondly, it's not

against the rules. I'm fairly certain you orchestrated this in defence of yourself, somehow.'

She smirked. 'Not orchestrated. Just told my brother that this hasn't been the best time for me. His guilt did the rest.'

'Fifty points,' he said, pride surging inside him. Not only because she'd been honest with her brother, but because Jaden had actually done something about it. Their talk must have helped.

'You know this puts me ahead now, right?' she said.

'One-thirty for you, one-twenty for me?' When she lifted her brows, he shrugged. 'I've been keeping track, same as you.'

They were walking behind the rest of the group. Jaden and Leela were far in the front—arguing, no doubt. When they all reached the line to enter the carnival, things went eerily silent. And then Tiff turned around and began asking Noah about his travels.

He could feel Ava stiffen next to him, and his annoyance at his ex trying to make conversation with him—*flirting* with him—was kidnapped by another emotion: satisfaction. Ava was *jealous*.

He immediately took a step back so that Ava was between him and Tiff, and deliberately included her in the conversation. Though it would have been worth it based solely on the fact that Ava relaxed as soon as he did so, it also managed to annoy Tiff. As soon as they got inside the carnival, she and Ken went their own way.

'Should I ask?' Jaden said, looking pointedly at Tiff's back.

'You could,' Noah replied, 'but I don't think it's going to get you any bonus points with your fiancée.'

Jaden glanced back to Leela with a grimace. She was at the bar, and when she turned they saw she'd ordered a large beer. Which she then downed.

'Yeah, she's not happy about this.'

'Why would she be?' Ava asked. 'You *knew* this wasn't going to go well for you. With her, I mean. You have no idea what it means to me.'

She stood on her tiptoes and kissed Jaden's cheek, and the affection and gratitude in her action did something to Noah's insides.

He and his father had never been overly affectionate with one another. They'd showed their love through spending time together. Doing things together. Which explained why, when Noah had told Kirk he was moving back home, his father's reaction hadn't been what he'd hoped for.

But he knew he couldn't have expected no consequences for leaving. He'd found that out the hard way with Ava. And now he'd found it out with his father. But they were dealing with it. Just as they were dealing with the aftermath of their first real conversation about how his mother's actions had affected them. And how his father's subsequent relationships had affected Noah.

Lunch had been a real hoot.

'I know I should have warned her,' Jaden was saying, 'but it was a spontaneous decision.'

'Clearly,' Noah commented. 'Though not a bad one.'

'Tell that to my future wife.'

'What you *can* tell your future wife,' Ava said, 'is that you're going to fold all those boxes by yourself in apology. And then you can drop them at my house tomorrow and I'll fold them for you.'

Jaden brightened, but then frowned. 'You have work until Friday, Ava. You can't fold a hundred and thirty boxes by yourself.'

'The office is quiet this time of year,' Ava replied easily, though Noah could tell that wasn't true. 'Besides, I can sleep after the wedding. And unless you want to fold those boxes yourself, so that you can a) make sure there *is* a wedding, and b) get your wife to sleep in the same bed with you afterwards—or before— you'll take me up on the offer.'

'I won't argue with that.' He kissed Ava on the forehead. 'Now—damage control.'

'Don't let her get too drunk!' Ava called after him, and Jaden glared at her when Leela looked over.

'You're enjoying this, aren't you?' Noah asked.

'The fact that I'm no longer going to have to pretend to be happy while folding boxes or the fact that we're here?'

'I was talking about how you're treating Jade, but, yeah, I guess the other two reasons work.'

She angled her head. 'I'm not going to lie and say I'm not enjoying how this is turning out for Jaden. But I feel like he deserves some of it—and that it's about time.' She shrugged. 'I'm only human.'

Noah smirked. 'Aren't we all?'

They began walking together, and he couldn't help but think what a perfect date it would have been under other circumstances. The carnival rides lit up the entire rugby field of the high school, and the Christmas theme meant that there were assorted Christmas characters running around. There were a couple of elves, a couple of reindeer, and all the stalls had workers wearing red Christmas hats.

It was ideal for someone who loved Christmas. For someone like Ava. But he needed to remember it *wasn't* a date. And that the only reason Jaden wasn't walking with them was because he had his fight with Leela to worry about.

So he'd use this opportunity of being alone with Ava constructively, and take his father's advice: he'd face the consequences of what had happened.

'Listen, about the night of the rehearsal dinner—'

'No,' she interrupted him.

'What?'

'My brother has put his relationship on the line to give me tonight.'

'I think that might be an exaggeration.'

'I don't,' she said solemnly, but her eyes twinkled. 'I'm not going to waste his sacrifice by talking about *that*. In fact, I'm sorely tempted to go find Tiff, just so that we can play the game again and I can beat you.'

'Now, we *both* know that's an exaggeration,' he said with a smirk.

'Yeah, you're probably right.' She tilted her head. 'Doesn't mean we can't still earn points, though.'

'How are you thinking of cheating now?'

'Not cheating,' she said haughtily. 'A bonus round, if you will.'

'I will.'

'You don't even know the terms.'

'Doesn't matter. I'm still going to win.'

'Ha! Well, now I'm tempted to tell you that you have to enter the carnival pageant.' Her eyes widened. 'Actually, that's been my plan all along.'

'Over my dead body.'

She sighed. 'I suppose you're right. There's no way you could enter and win it, thus winning the competition between us, too.'

He narrowed his eyes. 'The point of this competition is that we distract each other from the wedding.'

'And we can still do that.' She lifted her shoulders. 'Let's compromise, then, and say you'll win five hundred points if you enter the competition for at least one round.'

'What if I get through to the next round?'

'You'll get another hundred points. And so on. And so forth.'

After considering, he said, 'Fine. But you have to enter, too.'

She laughed. 'Oh, bring it *on*, Giles.'

CHAPTER EIGHTEEN

AVA WOULD READILY admit that entering a pageant because of a dare wasn't the smartest thing she'd ever done. But it wasn't the stupidest thing she'd done either. Not when her wedding, staying over at Noah's place and making out with Noah—numerous times—were all contenders for that title.

And certainly not when she added falling for Noah into the race.

Hell, entering the stupid pageant didn't even make the top ten.

As she went through the process of entering the competition it became clear which of those things *was* winning that title. Why else would she be challenging Noah to a competition? To enter the *pageant*? Why else would she be so determined to distract herself from that feeling in her stomach that told her how fast she was falling?

So she would enter the pageant. Even though

she hated the thought of going up there and having people ogle her. Even though her simple white dress couldn't compare to the beautifully patterned and coloured dresses of the women around her.

When she learnt that the women's pageant took place before the men's pageant, she told herself there was no point in complaining about it. *She'd* done this. And, regardless of how unsteady all of this—the pageant, her feelings— made her, she'd put on a show for Noah *and* the entire carnival.

She might as well.

'Contestant number seventeen—Ava Keller!'

Ava blew out a breath and then walked the length of the catwalk—shoulders back, legs slanting over each other, channelling the seven-year-old Ava who'd practised for this moment all the time. She heard cheering as she posed— from more than one person—and looked into the crowd to find the entire wedding party waving at her.

When her eyes landed on Noah's he gave her a wink and she narrowed her eyes, determined to find some way to get him back.

The only way she could think of to do it was to win the stupid pageant.

* * *

'I'm not sure how you convinced her to do this, but I am happy to pay you for it.'

Noah smirked, but it was more an act than anything else. He'd had no intention of having Jaden witness his humiliation, let alone Tiff and the others. But Jaden had found him, and had asked about Ava, and he hadn't been able to lie.

But now, seeing the look on Ava's face, he wished he had.

'Has she ever done anything like this before?' Leela asked.

She seemed to be better now—presumably because Jaden had told her he'd take care of the boxes.

Jaden shook his head. 'She didn't even want to take part in her school concerts.' His smile widened. 'I'm going to record this for posterity.'

He took out his phone, took a few pictures of Ava posing, and then chuckled to himself. 'Gold!'

They watched as she walked down the runway—pretty professionally, Noah thought, though he wasn't sure he was qualified to make that evaluation—and then Jaden asked, 'How *did* you manage to convince her to do this?'

'A bet.'

'A bet?' Leela repeated. 'She's doing this because of a *bet*?'

'Yeah. I mean, you know how she is.'

He hoped they did. Because he wasn't quite sure what he was talking about.

'It must have been some bet, man,' Jaden said with a quirked brow, his eyes sharp.

'Yeah. She and I have actually both entered tonight. Whoever gets furthest in the competition has to...' He paused, and then said the first thing that came into his mind 'Has to do a solo dance at your wedding.'

There was a long pause before Leela said, 'You mean *after* the formalities, when the dance floor is actually being used?'

'Of course,' he said immediately. 'It won't affect your wedding at all.'

'Well...' Jaden said after a moment. 'You'd better hope she wins. I've seen you dance.'

He pulled a face at Jaden, but his insides loosened in relief.

'I'm actually supposed to go out there and *speak* now?' Ava asked the man who'd brought her the bad news. 'I thought the extent of this was walking around and letting people judge me?'

'That's not how pageants work, ma'am.' He frowned. 'Didn't they tell you you'd have to speak when you entered?'

I wasn't paying attention.

'I don't think so, no.'

'Well, we have a pageant every night at the carnival to choose a carnival king and queen for that day. It isn't anything too demanding. You just have a couple of pictures taken with the crown,' he said, sounding almost bored. 'But the actual competition is judged on how much you entertain the crowd. You just go out there and introduce yourself. If they like you, you make it into the next round. That's a group dance—we teach you when you're out there, and it's more about having fun than anything else—and then in the final round you answer some questions. Got it?'

'Got it,' she said, but she felt dazed. All she could think about was that her fate in the stupid pageant was based on people *liking* her. 'I'm also pulling out.'

'What?'

'I'm sorry. I can't entertain people.' She gave the microphone back to him and stepped away. 'Trust me, you don't want me out there.'

She didn't give him a chance to reply, and

instead took a route back to her car where she knew no one would see her.

She sat there for a moment, breathing hard and fast, and then she drove the short distance back to Jaden's house. She used her spare key to get in, scribbled a note for him, and then transferred the unmade boxes to the car.

And then she went home, messaged Noah that she was okay—and Jaden, too, for good measure—and switched off her phone. And cuddled with her cat.

'She's pulled out.'

Everyone in their small group looked at Noah, but Jaden responded first. 'What do you mean, she's pulled out?'

'I mean she just sent me a message saying that I've won the bet and she's gone home because she isn't feeling well.'

Jaden took out his phone, blew out a breath. 'She sent me a message, too. But mine just says that she isn't feeling well so she's left. I'll call her.'

Noah let him do that, but he knew Ava wouldn't answer the phone. She wasn't the type to just run away. And she hadn't backed out because she wasn't feeling well. Something was wrong.

'Her phone's off. Maybe I should go see if she's okay?'

'She's fine,' Tiff said. 'I'm sure it's just stage fright. You don't have to spoil our evening because of her.'

'She's my sister,' Jaden said in a warning tone.

'Tiff's right, though.' Noah forced himself to say the words. 'I'm sure she's fine.'

'See?' Tiff said brightly, as if Noah's agreement somehow absolved her of any pettiness that had been in her answer. 'I told you.'

'I think I'll be off, too, though,' Noah said, trying hard not to clench his teeth. 'Early start tomorrow.'

'We literally just got here,' Tiff protested. 'Besides, we haven't had a chance to speak yet. We could—'

'No, thank you,' he interrupted. 'I'm happy to be in this wedding with you because of Jaden and Leela, but that is the only reason we're seeing each other now. If I had my way I would never have had to see you again after what happened. I'll see you all later.'

He'd almost reached the exit before Jaden caught up with him.

'That was...*intense*.'

'Yeah, sorry.' Noah exhaled. 'I just don't understand why she keeps trying to talk with me.'

'Because she's a human being who regrets what she did when she was just a kid.'

'She's told you that?'

'Yeah.' He grimaced. 'We've been friends for a while now. I didn't want to tell you—'

'Because you didn't want to upset me.' Jaden nodded. He blew out another breath. 'Look, I get that. And I'll apologise for embarrassing her, but I don't regret saying what I said.'

'You don't want to talk to her? You don't want closure?'

'I don't *need* closure. Not from her. Maybe after what she did—' He broke off, shook his head. 'I wasn't in love with her. Or I was, but it wasn't… I don't know. Complete.'

Jaden didn't reply for a moment. Then, 'Is it complete now?'

He didn't have to say that he was talking about Ava.

'I—' Noah cleared his throat. Stood taller. 'I think so.'

'You'd better know what you're doing.'

I have no idea. 'I do.'

'Be sure,' Jaden warned, his lips stiff, as though saying the words cost him something.

'She's been through enough.' He gritted his teeth. 'And I've made it worse.'

'She's already forgiven you,' Noah replied after a beat. 'She wouldn't be doing any of this if she hadn't.'

'Which makes me feel worse.' Jaden rubbed a hand over his face. 'Please, Noah, don't make me have to punch you. I have a lot of repressed anger that she didn't let me take out on her ex.'

'Understood.'

'And don't make me regret that you're back.'

His mouth curved. 'Can't guarantee that.'

Jaden's lips curved, too, though just a little. 'I guess it wouldn't be fair to ask. Not when I regretted your existence long before you even left.'

Noah laughed.

When the doorbell rang, Ava ignored it and snuggled closer to Zorro. Her cat was in one of his rare affectionate moods and was allowing her to put her arms around him. Not tightly enough to squeeze him, but enough to make the throbbing in her chest ease. She wasn't going to answer the door and mess that up.

But soon the ringing of the doorbell turned into a persistent knocking. And when the knocking became a pounding, Ava sighed and took a slow walk to the front door.

'What?' she said the moment she opened it.

Her heart swelled when she saw Noah, but then she remembered she could never be with him and it deflated almost as quickly.

'I could ask you the same thing,' he said, pushing past her into the house. 'Except I'd add "the hell" to the "what" to get my meaning across more clearly.'

She closed the door. 'Why don't you just say "what the hell?" then? It would sound a lot better than what you just said.'

'Fine. What the hell, Ava?'

'Actually, maybe it *was* better the other way,' she said, and lowered herself onto her couch. 'I could have just pretended I didn't know what you meant and sent you on your way.'

'Ava,' he said, his voice soft now. 'What's wrong?'

'Nothing. Fine,' she said when he gave her a look. 'Nothing that I have the energy to tell you about.'

'What happened at the carnival?'

'I told you, I don't have the energy to talk about—'

'Please.'

His tone had gone from soft to insistent, but it was the concern in that insistency that had her eyes filling.

She took a deep breath, and then stood up when it didn't make her feel any better. 'Tea?'

'No, thank you.' He paused. 'And you don't want tea either, Ava. You just want the distraction.'

'I *need* the distraction,' she said, and went to the kitchen before he had the chance to reply.

He didn't say anything as she made the tea, and the silence felt awkward. But he was there, she thought. And she took a moment to figure out how that made her feel.

It had been a long time since she'd had a rough night and someone had been there for her. She usually dealt with those nights alone, and once she was feeling stronger she'd visit Kirk. Or her brother, or her parents.

But having Noah there filled something inside her. And she'd forgotten what that felt like. Not to have to pretend. To want—despite how much she denied it—to talk. And not just to anyone—to *Noah.* It had always been Noah.

Damn it.

She hung her head as the kettle sounded, and could barely bring it up again so she could finish making her tea. She stirred the liquid for much longer than it required, and when she left the kitchen saw that Noah now sat on the seat she'd vacated, watching her.

Unwilling to think about whether he'd seen her have that moment in the kitchen, she set the tea down, sat and curled her feet under her body, and then waited for him to speak.

'I know what you're doing,' he said.

'Yeah? What?'

Please tell me because I have no idea.

'You're waiting for me to ask you what's wrong again.'

Her lips curved. 'You've always known me better than I've ever given you credit for.'

'Maybe not always,' he corrected her with a small smile. 'I think I've lost some of my ability since I left.' He paused. 'Help me to regain it.'

She looked down at her hands, watched as her fingers traced the lines of her palms as if she weren't the one controlling their movement.

'I don't know what went wrong. Or when.' Her fingers stilled, and then began to move again. 'I think I was too young when I met him. He was, too. We had ideas about who we wanted to marry and who we wanted to be, but when push came to shove neither of us were those people. Not for ourselves. Not for each other.'

'Ava,' he said slowly, on an exhalation of breath. 'Your life for the past seven years wasn't only tied to him. You've graduated since I last saw you. You have a successful career. Your family loves and supports you.'

'Those things aren't who I am. They're what I've achieved. And my family—' She exhaled sharply. 'They don't see the version of me who failed at my relationship. I mean, now they do, because I'm forcing them to. Because my quirky personality has turned surlier than usual and they have to tiptoe around me.'

'No one is tiptoeing around you.'

'*Everyone* is tiptoeing around me.' She threaded her fingers together. 'Jaden didn't speak to me about proposing to Leela until after he did it. And then, when they announced their engagement, they both glanced at me, checking to see how I would react. The pressure of that...' She shook her head. 'Trust me, I've been here this past year. I *know* how my family's behaviour towards me has changed.'

'And what about *your* behaviour?' he asked

after a moment. 'I'm not talking about the surliness—we knew about that before, and we loved you for it. I'm talking about the fact that you've turned into this…this *unsure* person. That you don't trust yourself. That isn't you. You used to be the most self-assured person I knew.'

'Oh, no, that was just pretending. I was much too in love with you to show you I wasn't completely confident in myself.'

'You were…you were *in love* with me?'

Her mouth curved into a smile he'd never seen before. Shy, insecure, seductive. How could that even be a combination? he wondered. Or was that description just an indication that he was totally enthralled?

'Don't pretend you didn't know.'

'I *didn't* know. Trust me, if I'd known—'

'You would have what?' she interrupted. 'Kissed me? Freaked out? Moved away? Stayed away for the past seven years?'

'That's not fair.'

'But it's not untrue.'

'I didn't leave because of what happened between us.'

'Not entirely, no. But it was factored into your decision.'

She leaned forward, picked up her cup of tea. Gripped it between her hands. Why did it feel as if she was gripping his heart there, too?

'Though, of course, you won't give yourself the chance to think about the real reasons you left.'

'I *have* thought about them.'

'Have you, though?' She tilted her head. 'After everything that's happened over the last weeks?'

He narrowed his eyes, wondering what he'd done to put her in this mood. And then he remembered that she'd been in the mood before he'd got there, and because he'd been determined to check whether she was okay he'd put *himself* in this position now.

But that didn't mean he deserved this line of questioning. He didn't need to delve into his motivations for leaving—or his motivations for the other decisions he'd made in his life—any more than he already had.

Because for the past two weeks he'd done nothing *but* that.

Because of her.

She'd reminded him that his father was

human. Imperfect and human. Noah hadn't seen that before he'd left. Then, he'd wanted to leave because he hadn't wanted to see his father heartbroken any more. He hadn't wanted to witness the pattern of it. Especially after his relationship with Tiff had shocked him into realising he might repeat that pattern, too.

But now Ava's words made him consider something else. Something that fitted now that he saw how his mother's cheating had affected him. He'd gone from being heartbroken over a cheating girlfriend to kissing Ava and feeling something for her within weeks.

He'd seen the pattern take root. He'd seen himself becoming his father. Being cheated on and then quickly moving from one relationship to the next. It had screwed with him. He could see that now. And it had forced him into ignoring the fact that what had happened with Ava hadn't been the same as his father's relationships.

But he'd been scared. The cheating and his feelings for Ava and everything to do with his mother and father had somehow meshed and he'd been *terrified*. Terrified of what Ava had made him want.

A relationship. A future. Things he hadn't

thought he could commit to. Things he'd been scared to face. And so he'd run.

'How did you know?' he asked her quietly.

'Because we're something,' she said simply. 'And you told me about how your father's choices made you feel.' She paused. 'And about your mother.'

Noah swallowed and wished he'd accepted the tea so that he'd have something to distract himself with. As he'd known she would, she let the silence extend. She was waiting for him to speak.

'The thing with Tiff... It shocked me.'

'Why?'

'Because I fell in love. Quickly. Stupidly. I ignored logic and I fell in love.'

'It happens to all of us.'

'But it shouldn't have happened to *me*. Not after what I'd seen with my father—' He cut himself off. Sighed. 'My father's relationships have bothered me my entire life. Because of their instability, yes, but also because I hated seeing my father hurt. That's one side of it.'

He lifted a hand, and then dropped it before he could do anything with it.

'The other side of it is I knew my mother had hurt him. And by doing that she hurt me with what she did, too—even though I only realised the truth of it after she died.'

He leaned forward, ran a hand through his hair.

'What happened with Tiff was like a perfect storm of…of *everything*.'

'The relationship moved fast, like your father's relationships. And then the cheating—'

'And you,' he interrupted, before he lost his nerve. 'Our kiss happened so quickly after Tiff—'

'And you thought you were turning into your father?'

He gave a curt nod. 'So I left.'

A long pause followed his words. 'You ran from it?' she asked softly.

He nodded again. 'And I called my *father* weak.'

'You're not weak. Neither of you are. You've both just had to deal with something tough.' She paused. 'But you can't run from it, Noah. It won't matter how far you go, or how hard you try to distract yourself. The fear, the pain… It stays with you.'

'Speaking from experience?'

'Yeah.' She lifted a shoulder. 'After I fell apart I tried to put myself back together again.

But no matter how hard I tried, it didn't change the fact that some of the pieces had broken—had shattered—during the process. I'm still me—' she gave him a sad smile '—but there are some parts missing.'

'He stole them.'

She shook her head, and then she set the tea down and brought her knees up to her chest. Her position did something to him, and he was standing before he knew it, pushing her tea aside and sitting on the table opposite her.

'What is it? What are you not telling me?'

She shook her head again, and desperation—fear—made his tone insistent.

'Ava, I can't help you if I don't know.'

'You *do* know, Noah. I've told you—' She drew in a ragged breath. 'He didn't steal anything from me. He just saw what I couldn't—what I didn't before. That I'm…too much to be loved.'

CHAPTER NINETEEN

'YOU CAN'T BELIEVE THAT.'

His disbelieving tone soothed Ava's heart, but a louder, stronger voice soon sounded over it.

If you were lovable—if there wasn't anything wrong with you—why did Milo leave? And why didn't Noah stay?

'I'm not upset about it,' she said, lowering her legs and straightening her shoulders. She'd had enough of the self-pity. 'I'm glad I know. Now I don't have to set myself up for failure. I can adjust my expectations.'

She stood now, and tried to move away. When he did the same it brought their bodies close together. She didn't want to feel the spark being close to him always brought. She didn't want to be reminded of the expectations she'd once had for the two of them. The expectations she'd admitted to him and he'd brushed off.

'That's the worst thing I've ever heard.'

'It's the truth.' She forced herself to look him

in the eyes. Accepted the quivering of her stomach as she did so.

'It's not the truth. You're not "too much". And, while we're at it, there's nothing wrong with you either. You're kind and sweet. I mean, it's under a couple of layers of other stuff,' he said when she opened her mouth. 'The surliness and the fire. But you wouldn't have agreed to be in Jaden's wedding if there wasn't something sweet and considerate inside you. You wouldn't have offered to fold these boxes—' he gestured to the cardboard she'd almost forgotten on the floor '—if you weren't a good sister.'

She didn't reply, lost in the longing for it to be as simple as he was making it out to be. But she wasn't the person he was describing. Or she *was*, but the balance was off. She was more surly than sweet. More blunt than kind.

She hated that those things came into her mind in the form of Milo's words. In the form of the expression on his face when he'd told her he didn't want to spend the rest of his life trying to avoid being snapped at. Or walking through it on eggshells because he was afraid of what she'd say.

'You don't believe me?' he asked.

'Because your perception is skewed. You... you care about me.'

'I do.' His voice was heavy with an emotion she didn't understand. 'Which is why you *should* believe me.'

'It's why I *don't* believe you. You're just like my parents. And, if I'm honest with myself, like Jaden, too. He gives me a hard time, but I know he loves me exactly as I am. And because of it he, my parents, and now you don't see me as someone who isn't perfect.'

He stared at her, and then laughed softly. 'You're not *perfect*, Ava.'

She frowned. 'Yeah, I know. I just said that.' But she hadn't expected him to agree.

'You *are* surly. And you're annoying. You needle me like no other woman I've met before. And your mouth is so sharp...' He lifted a hand, brushed his thumb over her lips as his other arm slid round her waist. 'And I wouldn't have wanted you so much if you were any different.'

And then he kissed her, and Ava's protests— her confusion—were engulfed by the emotions of that kiss.

His lips moved gently against hers, his tongue slipping between them. His hand moved from her waist up to her face, and it took her a moment to realise that he held her face in both his hands now. And that the embrace was as tender, as moving, as his kiss. She nearly wept.

Instead, she put her arms around his neck and told herself to fall into his light. She wished she'd put up her Christmas tree—wished she'd had the courage to celebrate the holiday she loved—so that the mental picture she'd always have of this moment would include Christmas. So that it would replace the broken picture she had of it now. Of Milo running from her. Of his face—ugly and twisted, and not the face of the man she knew—and his anger.

Determined to wipe it away, she pressed closer to Noah. And then she let her hands run over his body. The broad curves of his shoulders, the strength of his back. The slope between the bulge of his pecs, the valley between his abs. His body was the most extraordinary thing she'd ever touched, its lines and its curves a gift from heaven itself.

But the gift couldn't be for her. Even if he wanted to give it to her.

He felt the change in her and pulled back, hoping he hadn't crossed the line. But when he saw her face he realised that the line had been erased. No, that she was *about* to erase it. His heart jumped to his throat.

'You don't want this, Noah. Not really.'

Her breathless tone made the words all the more hurtful.

'You don't know what I want.'

'You don't either,' she said sadly. 'You think you want me because you want my body. But I can't—'

She broke off, shook her head. And then she cleared her throat and looked him dead in the eye.

Fire.

He was so in love with her.

'I can't give you my body without giving you more. And you don't want more.'

'Ava—'

'No, please, don't make this worse.' Despite the fire, her voice caught. But she didn't look away. 'Unless you're going to tell me that you're suddenly someone who wants to settle down. Who wants to stay in one place, buy a house—not as an investment, as a *home*—and raise kids, don't bother lying to me.'

'I didn't… I thought you didn't want that.'

'I was going to get married.'

He almost smiled at the roll of her eyes.

'Of *course* I want that.' She paused, and again her voice hitched slightly. 'Just because I think there's something wrong with me doesn't mean I believe I don't deserve that.'

'You do deserve it,' he said softly, urgently.

But he didn't say what he thought next.

Do I?

He'd spent all his life judging his father's choices. Blaming his father for his decisions. Ignoring the way Kirk had been affected by a cheating wife. Ignoring the way *he'd* been affected by it.

He'd used teenage heartbreak as an excuse to run away from it all. And now he was back. Older, and thoroughly chastised for being so unforgiving of his father's imperfections.

He'd make up for it now that he was back home. He and his father had already started at their lunch the other day. But he was less certain that he could move past the fear of relationships that seemed lodged inside him. And, though he wanted to with all his might, he was afraid to let go of the control. He was afraid to fall. To let himself be hurt.

If anyone could help him overcome the fear it would be Ava. He felt it in a deep part of himself that was only complete when he was with her. But she didn't deserve a man who was still figuring it out. And he didn't deserve the sweetness and the fire of her as he tried.

It wasn't that he didn't want more. It was that he couldn't give *her* more.

'I know I deserve it,' Ava said again after a moment. 'Which is why I'm going to ask you to leave.'

She shook her head when he opened his mouth and he stopped, unsure of what he would have said anyway.

So he left, and tried to figure out how he'd gone from avoiding relationships to wanting one so badly it hurt.

It was progress, she thought. Figuring out that she deserved to have the things she'd always wanted even though she wasn't perfect.

I wouldn't have wanted you so much if you were any different.

No, no, no. She was *not* going to spiral down that hole again. She'd spent days thinking about it. Nights. And it had had more of an effect on her than being jilted at the altar.

But now wasn't exactly the time to think about that. There must be some rule forbidding members of a wedding party from thinking about the possibility of the groom or bride being jilted. Especially on the day of the wedding.

Though there was no rule that said someone who *had* been jilted shouldn't be afraid of walking down an aisle again, even if they weren't getting married.

'Can you give me a moment alone?' Leela asked with a nervous smile, pressing a hand to her stomach.

Photographs had been taken, the groom and groomsmen were in place, and they were now only waiting for some of the guests to arrive before Leela and Jaden would make their vows.

'Yes, of course,' she said.

She and Tiff headed to the door, but Ava stopped as Leela called her back. She heard the door click behind her as she turned.

'This is probably not the best timing, but I wanted to tell you how sorry I am.'

Ava frowned. 'For what?'

'All of it. Forcing you to be a part of this.' She lifted a shoulder, offered a smile. 'You look gorgeous, though.'

Ava looked down at the navy blue lace dress and smiled back. 'Thank you. So do you. Though you don't need to hear that from me again.'

Leela's Cinderella-type wedding dress took up a significant amount of space in the room they'd got ready in, and Leela looked breathtaking in it.

'Thank you.'

'You're welcome.'

There was a pause.

'You didn't force me into this. I agreed. It was my choice.'

'I shouldn't have made you choose, though. I guess I got so swept up in wanting a Christmas wedding that I didn't give myself a chance to consider how much I could be hurting you. It wasn't until Jaden—' She broke off. 'I didn't tell him I was going to ask you to be a bridesmaid. I thought I'd surprise him because he loves you so much. He told me that I shouldn't have done it, and by then it was too late to take it back.'

'Thank you,' Ava said quietly. And felt the resentment she'd held for her brother—and for Leela—over the whole mess fade. 'I know I would have regretted letting Milo rob me of this moment if I hadn't agreed to it.' *Like he robbed me of so much else.* 'I'm glad you asked me. It's been hard, but it's been worth it.'

They smiled at each other, and then Leela let out a shaky breath. 'I'm so glad we're on the same page. I didn't want to enter my new family with the possibility of conflict lingering.'

Ava laughed. 'Oh, you're going to be a breath of fresh air for us. We don't talk about our issues,' she elaborated. 'In fact, I'm pretty sure if the roles were reversed Jaden would have carried this apology—and the admission—to the grave.'

'Oh, that'll change.' Leela winked at Ava. 'I have time.'

Ava left Leela alone then, joining Tiff outside.

'So,' Tiff said after a moment. 'You and Noah, huh?'

'No.' Ava frowned. Shook her head. 'No.'

'Yeah, you sound like you're telling the truth.' Tiff smirked when Ava looked over at her. 'Noah's father was…er…*entertaining* a friend of mine the night of the rehearsal dinner. At the dam, wasn't it?'

Hating that her skin was heating, Ava cleared her throat. 'Just a swim.'

'Sure.' There was a beat of silence. Then, 'I think part of the reason I did what I did was because I knew Noah didn't want me.'

'Oh, no. We don't have to talk about this.'

'I know.' Tiff smiled, and for the first time

Ava thought it was genuine. 'But I guess I'm tired of being the bad guy. And of being jealous of you.'

'Bad guy—jealous? Of *me*?'

Tiff rolled her eyes. 'See, this is exactly what I'm talking about. The fact that you don't know how feisty and charming you are is *so* annoying. And then there's your face...' Tiff shook her head, but winked at her. 'Sickening.'

'I... I don't understand.'

'Noah never looked at me the way he looked at you, Ava. The way he *looks* at you.' Tiff's face tightened. 'I guess... I guess I was looking for someone to look at me that way. So I did something stupid—and I've done more, I promise you—and eventually I realised why. *Eventually*,' she said, tilting her head, 'meaning last week at the carnival.'

'I honestly don't know what to say.'

'So don't say anything.' Tiff shrugged. 'Or, no—do. Tell Noah I'm sorry. He'll believe it if it comes from you.'

And then they were being told the ceremony could start, and there was no more time to think about the bombshell Tiff had just dropped.

It was one of the worst things she'd ever done, walking down an aisle again. It didn't matter that it wasn't the aisle she'd walked down on her wedding day. It was just the *familiarity* of it. And the sympathy she felt coming from her side of the family.

It nearly caused her to stumble. But then she saw Kirk, and he nodded at her with a slight smile. And though her legs were still shaky she felt steadier.

And then her eyes met Noah's.

There was something on his face that made her want to cry. But not because he was looking at her in pity. No, it was because he was looking at her as if he *saw* her. *Her.* The woman who'd grown up and taken chances. Who'd been bold enough to ask her brother's best friend to kiss her. Who'd eavesdropped on conversations. Who was fierce and honest and blunt.

He didn't look at her and see a failure. He didn't look at her and see what he needed to change.

I wouldn't have wanted you so much if you were any different.

And when her legs went wobbly this time, it had nothing to do with the fact that she'd walked down the aisle before. It was because she wanted to do it again. And this time she wanted to be walking towards Noah.

CHAPTER TWENTY

'I'M GOING TO regret this,' Noah said. 'I'm going to wake up every night for the rest of my life and regret this.'

'But hopefully this will mean you'll wake up every night next to Ava and you'll be able to entertain yourself!' Leela grinned when she saw Jaden's face. But mercifully—for all involved—she stopped talking.

'When did you become like this?' Jaden asked with a shake of his head. But he curved an arm around his wife's waist and nuzzled her neck.

'About four hours ago,' Leela said with a giggle. 'It came with the title of Mrs Keller.'

'Ooh, what else—'

'Please,' Noah begged. 'Don't make this worse than it already is.'

'Don't take your emotions over this stupid grand gesture out on us.'

'You need to talk me out of this.' He turned to Jaden. 'Tell me you don't want me to be with your sister. Tell me that I shouldn't do this and ruin your wedding.'

'I *don't* want you to be with my sister,' Jaden told him. 'But you can't ruin the wedding. Most of it's done, and I got what I wanted.'

He smiled at Leela, then turned back to Noah.

'Again, just so that it's clear: I don't want you to be with my sister. But...but you make her happy,' he said reluctantly. 'I've seen her smile more in the last two weeks than I have in the last year. Maybe even before that.' He paused. 'And since you've been back, I've also learnt more about how she's feeling than I have in the last year. So, you know...' Jaden shrugged.

It was as much approval as Noah was going to get, and it warmed his heart—before he remembered what he was planning on doing.

'That doesn't change the fact that Ava's going to hate it. I'm going to embarrass her. Just like at her own wedding.'

'You're right. There probably *is* a chance she's going to hate it. And that she'll be annoyed that she's being embarrassed in front of her family again.'

'Wow. Thanks.'

'There's also a chance that she might *not* be embarrassed,' Jaden continued. 'There's a chance that she might love it and accept that you're in love with her.'

He rolled his eyes and Noah laughed.

'Besides,' Leela said, 'maybe you need to balance the bad embarrassment with the good kind.'

'There's a *good* kind?'

'Well,' Jaden said as they got a signal from the band, 'you're about to find out.'

With unsteady legs Noah made his way towards the band. He was still pretty sure he was going to regret what he was about to do, but he wanted to show Ava that he was serious about what he was going to tell her.

He winced when the singer handed him the microphone and he remembered he wasn't going to *tell* her anything.

'Excuse me, everyone,' Noah said.

The entire crowd looked at him, but he soon found the face of the only person he really cared about.

'I have something to say, and I have the bride and groom's permission, so I'm not stealing anyone's thunder.'

He saw Ava glance at Jaden and Leela—Jaden nodded at his sister and Leela blew her a kiss—before she turned back to him with a frown.

What are you doing? she mouthed, but he only shook his head, and continued speaking into the microphone.

'You see, today's been a bit of a rough day for some of us here. Particularly for some of the people in the wedding party.' Ava's eyes widened, and she shook her head at him. 'And I'm not ashamed to admit that I'm one of them.'

He took a step off the platform where the band was playing and walked into the crowd. And then he took a deep breath, because he didn't think there would ever be anything more terrifying than confessing his feelings in front of over a hundred people.

'You see, for the longest time I was afraid of falling for anyone. I had commitment issues, and I had a lot of excuses as to why.'

He took his eyes off Ava for a moment to look for Tiff, and nodded at her. Then he found his father and gave him a small smile.

'The truth is, I was afraid of being hurt. And having feelings for someone—real, deep feelings—terrified me even more. So I ran.'

Now he looked back at Ava.

'But I'm tired of running. You make me want to stand still, Avalanche. You always have.'

With another breath he turned back to the band and nodded.

'And now I'm going to win *all* the points to prove it to you.'

The band began to play.

He was a terrible singer. He was a less terrible dancer. And all in all it made Noah's performance well worth the thousand points needed to win the game.

She bit her lip to keep from laughing as he belted out a note that had the whole room cringing, and then didn't bother when he did a little jiggle to accompany it. In that moment it didn't matter that she was fairly sure Noah had lost control. It only mattered that she was laughing, and that for the first time in a year she didn't care that people were looking at her.

He walked towards her, taking her in his arms and giving her a twirl before bringing her up against him. The song ended, and his face crinkled into a smile, but she saw the nerves.

'A thousand points,' she told him breathlessly. 'You win fair and square.'

'Yeah?' His smile widened. 'That's great.'

'Oh, yes. *Especially* since the videographer got it for the wedding video.' She nodded over to the woman, who winked at them with a smile.

He groaned. 'I *knew* I was going to regret this.'

'You shouldn't,' she said, her heart hammering. 'It was—' She cut herself off, decision made. 'Why don't I show you?'

She pulled his head in for a kiss, and heard applause and cheers from her family. Having no desire to give them a show—other than the one they'd already had anyway—Ava pulled back almost immediately and angled her head in acknowledgment to the crowd.

Noah grinned at her, and then handed the microphone back to the singer of the band before taking her hand. 'Can we go somewhere to talk?'

'We probably should.'

And just like that she was brought out of the little bubble of joy she'd been in since he'd started speaking into that microphone.

It was still light outside, the sky soft with orange and yellow as the sun made its way to the horizon. It made the vineyard look soft, too—the vines, the abundance of grapes, the green hills and slopes in the background. Romantic. Beautiful. The perfect setting for a promise of for ever.

'Did you really like it?'

They were on the balcony overlooking the vineyard now, far enough away from the reception that they had privacy.

'I loved it.' She rested her forearms on the railing, let out a breath. 'Though I'm still trying to figure out why you'd do it.'

'You know why.' There was a pause. 'Hell, every single person in that venue knows why.'

'Yeah.'

She dipped her head and told herself that now wasn't the time to cry. But even the thought of crying made her want to cry. She hadn't trusted anyone enough to cry in front of them since she was a little girl. She didn't know how many times she'd cried in front of Noah since he'd been back.

Quick and fast. Tell him and then get out of here and cry in peace.

'Today's been interesting.'

'What makes you say that?'

She laughed quietly. 'No need for sarcasm.' She paused as he mirrored her position on the balcony. 'What I mean is that it was harder than I thought it would be. But then there were moments when it was easier, too.'

You're not making any sense.

She cleared her throat. 'It was hard going through a wedding again. Up until Jaden and Leela were pronounced husband and wife I held my breath. Because last year up until that moment things were going pretty well for me, too.'

'He did it just before you said your vows?'

'Yes.'

He swore.

Her lips curved. 'It gets easier thinking about it. Or maybe not thinking about it, but talking about it.' She angled her body towards him. 'Or maybe it's just easier with you.'

She reached out, took his hand.

'Which is why some of today was easy, too. You didn't look at me like I was broken. You saw *me*, and I can't... I can't tell you how much that means to me.' She cleared her throat when emotion clogged there. 'So when I felt over-whelmed—when I struggled to breathe and my throat closed, when the tightness in my chest made me feel like I was going to snap— I looked for you. And even when you weren't looking at me you made me feel better.'

His hand tightened on hers. 'What does that mean?'

'It means—' She let the air of her lungs slowly as she prepared to say the words. 'I think it means I love you. And not in the silly teenage way I used to, but—'

Her next words were stopped by his kiss, and selfishly she let herself have it. If only for a moment.

'I love you,' he said.

'I know.' She wrapped her arms around his waist, rested her head on his chest and squeezed her eyes shut. And then she pulled back and took a step away from him, lifting a hand when he moved to come closer. 'I know you *think* that.'

'I think—' He frowned. 'No, I *know* that. I embarrassed myself in front of an entire room full of people. I'm taking this risk even though—' he broke off. 'I haven't done any of this because I *think* I love you.'

'Okay,' she said slowly, 'maybe I didn't phrase that properly. I meant that...that what you feel for me is probably—'

'Love,' he interrupted flatly. 'I *love* you.'

'You *can't* love me, Noah. You can only love a whole person and I'm not... I'm not whole.'

'And yet here I am, offering you my love.'

'And your commitment?' she asked. 'Are you ready to commit to me, too?'

His expression tightened. 'Yes.'

She bit her lip. 'I don't want you to feel you have to say that.'

'No, that's not it.' The hand he had on the railing tightened. 'I'm...*scared*, Ava. I'm scared of being hurt. I didn't realise I could be until Tiff, after all the stuff with my parents—' He let out ~n unsteady breath. 'If you picked up hesitation it's because of that—not because I don't want to be committed to you. It's the same thing that happened the other night when you asked me about it.' He paused. 'I *want* to be in a relationship. I want to settle down, build a home, have a family. With *you*. Because you make me want it. Even though it still terrifies me, you make me want to risk it.'

A heady sensation passed through her, settling in her chest, and it took her a moment to realise it was hope.

'Why didn't you just tell me that the other night?'

'Because I thought you deserved more than me.'

His hands dropped to his sides and then he put them in his trouser pockets and stared out at the vineyard.

'I only realised my mom's cheating had affected me this deeply recently. I didn't—' He broke off, clenched his jaw. 'I want to give you everything you deserve, Ava. And I thought that because I'm still figuring things out I wouldn't be able to.'

'I think,' she said slowly, after a beat, 'that you've forgotten you told me I'm not perfect. And if I'm not perfect—and we both know I'm not—why would you think you had to be perfect for me?'

She could almost see him trying to formulate an answer, but he didn't respond and she bit back a smile.

'And since we're talking about it,' she continued, 'you said you had commitment issues earlier. I don't agree. I mean, you've had a relationship with the most difficult person I know—and I still question your taste for being friends with my brother—for most of your life. And you tried with your father, too. You didn't agree with him and yet you made sure to stay in touch. To see him every Christmas. You and I have had a pretty long relationship, too.' She let it linger. 'All of our relationships are forms of commitment. Not only the romantic ones.'

The features of his face relaxed slowly and the side of his mouth curved. 'I don't know how much of that is true. But I'd like to find out. With you. If you'll have me.'

'I want to. I want *you*.' She exhaled slowly. 'But I can barely look at myself in the mirror right now. All I see is…is a woman who was left at the altar.'

'So see yourself through my eyes.' He took a step closer, held her hands in his. 'See yourself through the eyes of a man who loves you.'

'I have.'

'He didn't love you, Ava. Not like I do.'

'I want—' She broke off and found herself struggling against tears again. 'I want to believe you,' she said slowly, 'but it just feels like… *I* feel like… I can't,' she ended helplessly, when she couldn't formulate her thoughts, her emotions, coherently.

She wanted to say she didn't deserve him—but then he'd believe *he* didn't deserve *her*, and she knew that wasn't true.

So why was it so easy to believe it of herself?

'So all of this was for nothing, then?' he asked in a careful tone, letting go of her hands. 'Why try to convince me that I can be what you deserve—what you want—if you don't want me?'

'Of *course* I want you. I just—' Again she cut herself off. She couldn't explain it.

Silence stretched so far, so thinly between them that Ava wondered what would happen if it snapped. And then she watched as it did. When Noah ran a hand over his hair and walked back to the reception.

'I can't believe you agreed to this, Dad.' Noah's hand tightened on the steering wheel. 'You *know* how things ended between Ava and me and you still agreed to have Christmas with the Kellers. *And* you dragged me into your invitation.'

'You need to face it, Noah,' his father replied, just as he had before. 'You knew there was a chance this would happen, and you took that risk when you declared your love for your best friend's sister at his wedding.'

'Can you stop reminding me about that?'

'I've never been prouder,' his father said sombrely.

'So that's a no, then?'

Now Kirk grinned. 'Never.'

Noah grunted, and figured the only way he wouldn't rile himself up even more was if he kept quiet. He wasn't a glutton for punishment. He took no pleasure out of pain. And yet he'd agreed to attend the stupid Christmas party the Kellers were hosting, knowing it would be painful for him.

He'd returned to the reception at the wedding ready to put on the performance of his life. But when his feet had taken him directly to Jaden and Leela, and then to his father, and his mouth had told them that he was leaving, he'd realised he'd had his fill of performance for the day.

And so had Ava, it seemed, since Jaden had later told him—very sympathetically—she hadn't returned to the wedding either.

It had made things easier for them both, he'd realised when he'd thought about it. Because it would have seemed as if the two of them had escaped the wedding to be romantic. Which would have been his preferred ending to the day.

Instead he'd gone home feeling like a fool, and now he was being forced to see her again.

The Keller house was decorated as if the Wise Men themselves were coming to Christmas lunch. There was tinsel, stockings, Christmas elves, a giant, beautifully decorated Christmas tree, and a nativity scene. And outside on the porch—where he was informed they'd be eating—was a long table fully decked with red and green, along with the requisite Christmas crackers.

The lamb he and his father had brought had been taken out of his hands, a beer placed in them instead, and still he hadn't seen Ava. And of course he couldn't be the one to ask where she was.

'Surely it can't only be the four of us today?' Kirk asked, almost as if he'd heard Noah's thoughts.

'You're right,' Ruth Keller told him. 'Jaden and Leela are coming. They're picking up Ava on their way.'

'Why isn't she coming in her own car?' he heard himself ask, kicking himself as he did.

'Oh, I don't think she wanted to drive alone today,' Ruth told him kindly. 'This is difficult for her after last year. We've had to force her out of the house.'

'Oh.'

'You're surprised?' Ruth said after a moment. 'I'm sure that's because Ava's given you the impression that she's fine.'

'No, ma'am,' he said truthfully. 'She's never quite been able to do that with me.' He cleared his throat. 'I'm surprised because she's given me the impression that you and Uncle Sam aren't aware she's struggling.'

Ava's parents exchanged a look, and then Ruth said, 'Of course she has. That girl would eat her own limbs to make sure we're not in pain.' She sighed. 'I wish she would just be honest with us.'

'I think she thinks—' Noah hesitated, wondering if he was betraying Ava's confidence by telling them this. But then he saw the expression on Ruth's face and continued. 'She thinks it's *her* fault that the wedding was called off. And she doesn't want to tell you the truth about how it's been affecting her because she's afraid you'll think poorly of her.'

Ruth's face blanched; Sam's tightened. For a moment an awkward silence thrummed in the room. Then the doorbell rang—of course Ava would arrive *now*—which broke the tension.

'Thank you for telling us, Noah,' Ruth said quietly, nodding at Sam to get the door. 'And, for what it's worth, we think you and Ava would make a lovely couple.'

She got up then as well, and followed her husband inside.

'That's a hell of a thing you just did,' Kirk commented.

'Yeah. I just hope I didn't make things worse.'

'I don't think so.' There was a beat before Kirk continued, 'You know her better than anyone else does.'

Noah looked at his father with a frown, but there was no time to discuss it further. Jaden and Leela walked in first—looking appropriately loved up—followed by Ava.

Concern immediately flared inside of him at the sight of her pale face. At her strained expression. When she saw him her eyes lit, before going dim again. And when she gave him a slight nod and kissed his father on the cheek, Noah thought he heard his heart shatter in his chest.

* * *

One day Christmas would feel like it used to.

At least that was what she told herself.

There wouldn't be tension as everyone avoided talking about the elephant in the room. Last year it had been her wedding; this year it was her and Noah. There wouldn't be furtive glances at her. Those expressions of concern, of curiosity. And, in Noah's case, the complete avoidance of her.

She deserved it. But for a moment when she'd walked into the room she'd forgotten that she'd spoilt it all. She'd only remembered that they were in love and she'd felt that heady hope again. And then the memories had flooded back and she'd realised she'd only been fooling herself.

But some day Christmas would go back to being wonderful. She'd be happy again, and she'd feel festive. Her family's laughter wouldn't grate on her emotions; their happiness wouldn't make her ill with longing. It would just be a holiday she could spend with the people she loved and enjoy the festivity of it.

For now, she had alcohol.

'Maybe you should go easy on the champagne,' Jaden said as he joined her on the porch steps.

'I'm offended. This is only my third glass.'

'But you barely ate.' Jaden took the champagne from her and downed it, then handed her the empty glass. 'You're welcome.'

She grunted, and set the glass on the step next to her. He was right. And the whole alcohol thing had been more of a distraction than anything else.

'Why are you sitting out here alone with champagne anyway? Noah left an hour ago.'

'It's not about him.'

But it was. Partly.

'Ava,' Jaden said, in his *I'm your big brother* voice, 'I say this with the utmost love, but you have to stop feeling sorry for yourself.'

'Excuse me?'

He winced, but said, 'You heard me.' He waited a beat before he continued. 'It's been a year. Long enough for you to snap out of your self-pity.'

'I'm *not* feeling sorry for myself. And even if I were, who the hell are you to tell me I can't? You, with your perfect wedding and your brand-new wife?'

'I'm your brother.' He put an arm around her shoulders. 'And I love you. Which is why I can be honest with you.' He squeezed her shoulder, then pulled his hand back. 'Look, no one is saying that what happened last year didn't suck. It did. But you're using it as an excuse not to move on.'

'Because of Noah?'

'Yes.' He was unperturbed by her surly tone. 'And because after last year, you think there's something wrong with you.'

'Who told you that?' she asked sharply.

'Heard it through the grapevine.'

'Noah.'

'Actually, from Mom and Dad—the moment you were out of earshot.' He tilted his head. 'But they heard it from Noah.'

'I should never have told him.'

'I'm glad you did. We all are. Or we wouldn't have the chance to tell you that you're absolutely wrong if you think it's true.' He paused. '*And* that you're feeling sorry for yourself.'

She sucked in her lip as it wobbled. 'It *is* true.'

'Ava—'

'No, Jaden, it *is*. Milo told me—'

'Milo was selfish. He always knew you were too good for him and yet somehow he managed to make you believe it was the other way around.'

She blinked. And then took a very deliberate breath when the air simply vanished from her lungs.

'I don't know… I don't know what to say.'

'Don't say anything. Just believe it.'

There was a long pause while she tried to figure out how she *could* believe it. No, first she was trying to figure out whether her brother had always felt that way about her ex-fiancé. Had her parents felt the same? And, if so, why had none of them told her?

'You wouldn't have believed us if we'd told you.' Jaden's eyes crinkled when her head turned sharply, and he gave her a wry grin. 'I've known you for all of your twenty-five years, Ava. I know how your mind works.'

'Okay, as disturbing as that is, it isn't the most disturbing thing you've said to me today.' She paused. Exhaled. 'I wish you'd told me. It could have saved me a lot of heartache.'

'And then I'd have had to tell you "I told you so", and while I would have enjoyed it, I don't think you would have.' His lips curved, then his smile faded. 'It's something I'll regret all my life. I know what it's like to fall in love when you're young.' He paused. 'I think it was worse for you, because you were so determined to prove that that kiss I'd walked in on—' he shuddered '—between you and Noah didn't mean anything.'

'What is *happening*?' Ava asked, her eyes wide. 'Are you revealing every single thought you've ever had?'

'No. I'm just lifting the carpet we sweep all our opinions under.' He let out a breath. 'If anything I've said today isn't true, then by all means forget it. But I always thought you'd come to these realisations yourself. The fact that you haven't points to the whole feeling sorry for yourself thing.'

She sighed with a shake of her head. Paused to consider it. 'Maybe you're right and I *do* feel sorry for myself. But, freaking hell, my fiancé walked out on me at the altar. *Can't* I feel sorry for myself?'

'Of course you can. And you have,' he added. 'But if you let it interfere with this thing with Noah—' he rolled his eyes '—then maybe there *is* something wrong with you.'

Now she rolled *her* eyes. 'Ah, my ever-sensitive brother.'

'And my dorky—but perfect—little sister.' He kissed her on the cheek and then stood up. 'Now, take some time to think about your sins and then come inside and let Mom and Dad tell you exactly what I just did but in a nicer way.'

He took one step away, and then paused. 'And if you ever, *ever* make me advocate for a relationship between you and Noah again, please know that I will strangle you in the process.'

She laughed softly as he walked away, and then took a deep breath and watched as the sun began to lower behind the mountains she could see from her parents' house. Her eyes stayed there as her mind whirled. As she realised that Jaden had been right about her relationship with Milo.

She'd known they weren't right for one another, though she hadn't quite thought that she was better than him. But there had been signs that had pointed to how mismatched they were long before she'd realised it. Signs she hadn't given herself permission to see even after he'd left.

She was too strong-minded for someone like him. And maybe that was why she hadn't listened when her gut had told her they didn't fit.

She hadn't listened to it for five years. *Five years.* Even when there had been an extra flutter of panic in her chest as they'd approached the wedding she'd ignored it. She could see now that the fluttering had been warning her. And it had stayed with her after, saying the *I told you so* Jaden hadn't wanted to.

How, then, had she managed to turn it into a critique of who she was?

Because it had been easier, she realised. Easier to believe that Milo was right, that she needed to be fixed. That way she'd been able to nurture the hurt inside her. She'd been able to hold it close and use it as an excuse not to move on. Because if she didn't move on she wouldn't get hurt again.

It took some time for the realisation to settle inside her. And for her to figure out what it meant that she and Noah had the same fears about being in a relationship.

They each thought they didn't deserve the other. They were both scared of getting hurt. But he'd taken a chance and proclaimed his love for her nevertheless. He'd been brave and she hadn't.

But she wanted to be brave. Because now she understood that she couldn't wait for her fears to disappear. She'd be putting her life on pause again if she did wait. She'd figure it all out, just as Noah would. And she was determined that they'd figure it out together.

But first she had to go inside the house and face her parents. And then she had to convince her brother to get involved with her and Noah one more time…

CHAPTER TWENTY-ONE

WHAT *WAS* IT with the Keller family and trying to get him to celebrate with them? It was enough to make him consider leaving again.

But when his father's face popped into his mind—and he thought of the ease their relationship had slid into since they'd had that talk—he knew that it was an exaggeration. He was just miserable because he was in love. And the woman he loved didn't want to be with him.

His only consolation was that Ava wasn't going to be attending Jaden's New Year's Eve party. After the Christmas tension he didn't think they'd survive another occasion together. His stomach still felt jittery because of it, and it had almost nothing to do with how unhappy Ava had been.

Almost.

Was she unhappy because she wanted to be with me?

He pushed the thought to the back of his

mind. Thinking about that would do him no good now. Nor would remembering that light in her eyes when she'd first seen him.

No good. No good at all.

He pulled into the driveway at Jaden's house, and was surprised to see only three cars there. He recognised one as belonging to Jaden's parents, but the other two he wasn't sure about. Until he realised he'd seen them there before and groaned.

The rest of the wedding party. *Great.* Now Tiff would be able to see his unhappiness.

Not that it mattered, he told himself, getting out the car. He'd come to accept that his relationship with Tiff had been a teaching moment in his life. And he'd resented her more for his own reasons than for anything *she'd* ever done to him.

He needed to move on.

He thought he had.

He grunted at the unwelcome thought, and then rang the doorbell. He was surprised to see Tiff open it.

'Hi,' she said.

'Hi.' He waited as she stepped back, and then he moved past her. 'It's good to see you again.'

'It is?'

Her surprise made him feel guilty. Until it was replaced with confusion.

'Ah, she told you,' she said.

'I'm sorry?'

'Ava. She told you I was sorry.' She smiled at him. 'I told her you'd listen to her. But I'm still glad I have the opportunity to tell you in person. I'm sorry...about everything.'

It took him a moment to process all the information, but then he nodded. 'I'm sorry, too. For how I've handled things...since.'

'Great.'

'Great.'

There was a pause. Then, 'Well, you can just go through. Everyone is on the deck.'

After that surprising exchange, the rest of the night was uneventful. The conversation was easy for the most part, except for the unexpected mentions of Ava's name and the uncomfortable glances at him, which he ignored.

Half an hour before midnight his father strolled in.

'Dad?' He stood. 'What are you doing here?'

'I couldn't let the first New Year's Eve my son spends at home in seven years pass without us being together.' He slapped Noah on the back.

'So, what? You pitch up half an hour before midnight?' he teased, but he was pleased.

'Yeah, well… I had some things to take care of.'

He winked at Noah, and then the lights went out and a familiar song began to play.

Noah's jaw dropped when he saw Ava walk onto the deck.

She felt a new appreciation for the embarrassment Noah had put himself through at Jaden's wedding. Here, she was only performing in front of her family—and Tiff and Ken, though they didn't really count. But then, none of them did when she made eye contact with Noah.

Her cue came and she lifted the microphone Jaden had plugged into his sound system and began to sing the song Noah had sung to her at the wedding. It was a silly Christmas song, about Father Christmas and his elves, and when she'd been practising she'd realised that Noah had chosen the song because of the jokes they'd made with one another when she'd been staying at his place.

The singing had been easier to perfect than the dancing. She'd watched the video of Noah's performance that Kirk had recorded on his phone and graciously sent her over and over again, but some of the moves were Noah originals and hard to imitate. Not to mention the fact that she was wearing his firefighter uniform.

No one could accuse her of not going all out for love. She only hoped it would work.

She beguiled him—and heaven only knew why. Though he knew she was a good dancer, she couldn't move very well in his uniform, and his helmet kept falling over her face during the song.

But still she was beguiling. So much so that he only realised they were alone when the music stopped and she stood in front of him.

'Pretty decent show,' he commented. 'Not as good as mine, though. I'd give you nine hundred points.'

'I'm pretty sure that still makes me the—' She cut herself off as the helmet slipped over her face again.

Grinning, he took it off her head. 'You were going to say winner, and even my helmet knew you'd be lying.'

'Fair enough.' She paused. 'It wouldn't be the first time, I guess.'

'That my helmet knew you were going to lie?'

'That I lied,' she said, with a smile that turned his heart over.

'What do you mean?'

'I mean— What do you *think* I mean?' she asked. 'What do you *think* me getting your father to get me your firefighter's uniform and send me the video of you performing that ridiculous song so that I could perform it and also getting my brother to invite you to this party means?'

She was out of breath when her speech was over, and while she caught it his mind played catch-up.

'You're saying you planned this?'

She rolled her eyes. 'Duh.'

'Why?'

'Why do you *think*?'

He opened his mouth, then shook his head. 'That's not fair.'

'Really?' Her brow furrowed. 'Okay, fine. I love you, Noah, and I want to be with you.'

His stunned silence slithered into her chest and gripped her heart.

'What...what changed?'

She was prepared for this. She exhaled. 'I realised I was scared, too. Of not being what you deserve. Of being hurt. I couldn't bring myself to move on because of it.'

He didn't reply immediately. 'You know what I think?' His voice was quiet. 'We should stop getting in our own heads about this and just admit we deserve each other.'

She smiled, the pressure in her chest easing. 'I agree.'

He smiled back. 'I won't hurt you, Avalanche.'

'I know.' She lifted a hand to his cheek, and then dropped it. 'It's still terrifying. All of this is.' She slid her fingers into her hair, puffing out her curls where they'd been flattened by his helmet. 'Milo and I weren't right for one another. But…but I can't deny he made some good points.'

'Ava—'

'It's not just going to go away,' she said softly. 'These insecurities are here. The fears are, too. I have to work through them. But I won't let them keep me from being with you, if that's still what you want. Especially since my dear brother has reminded me of how getting into a relationship with the first man who was interested in me after you left might have been a sign of how much I was running away from my feelings for you.'

'I...' He dragged the sound out. 'I did *not* see that coming.'

She laughed. 'Neither did I. *Jaden* had to point it out.' She did a mock shudder. 'He wasn't happy about it.'

'I can imagine.' He let out a breath.

'It was easier for me to stop living,' she said after a moment. 'It meant I didn't have to get hurt again or do anything about the brokenness inside me.' She took a step forward, her heart hammering. 'But if you're willing to be patient as I put myself together again—properly this time—'

He cut her off with a kiss.

It was relief more than anything else, but he sank into the passion, the fire, the *home* of kissing her. And then he pulled back, told himself he needed to be sure.

'I don't want you to do this because when we're together things are awkward. We can go back to...to being friends.'

'I thought you said we weren't ever really friends?'

He acknowledged the hit with a nod. 'You know what I mean.'

'I do.' Her smile faded. 'I do miss you. And I don't want things to be awkward. But, more importantly, I love you and I want to be with you. It's that simple.' She drew in a breath. 'If that's still what you want.'

'It is.' He paused. 'If you're willing to be patient with me as I work through my own stuff.'

'For as long as it takes.' She smiled. 'Thank you for not drawing that out.'

'I wanted to.'

Her smiled widened, heating his insides. 'Can't blame you for it. I wanted to, too.'

'Except you didn't want to do it to someone you love.'

'I guess.' She lifted a hand, brushed his lips with her thumb. 'I wouldn't know.'

'Because you've never really been in love before?'

'Not like this, no.'

He slid his arms around her body, drew her closer. 'Me neither.'

They stood like that for a moment, and then she said, 'My brother must be hating having to watch this.'

'They're watching?'

'Every single one of them.' Her eyes shifted

to behind him, and then moved back to his face. 'Should we give them something to look at?'

'You mean besides the fireworks?'

As he said it, the first set of fireworks went off.

He smiled. 'Happy New Year, baby.'

'Happy New Year,' she replied, and pressed her lips to hers.

EPILOGUE

Two years later, Christmas Day

'LOOK, YOU OWE me this. I saved your life. It's the least you can do.'

Zorro stared at Noah, only one message clear in his eyes. *I hate you for doing this to me.*

Which was a fair point, Noah thought, amusing himself by playing with the bow around Zorro's neck. But then his phone beeped and his heart jumped into his throat.

Showtime.

He picked Zorro up, and thanked the cat for not resisting. Then he tentatively put the cat on the kitchen counter, which had now been cleared of the Christmas spread that had been there only a few hours ago.

He and Ava had hosted their families at his house this year. His father had come with his girlfriend—a woman he'd been dating for over a year now and was 'taking it slowly' with, as he'd told Noah—as well as Ava's parents, Leela and Jaden and their new bundle of joy.

Throughout the day Noah had watched Ava. Watched as she'd laughed, as she'd joked. He'd watched as she'd teased her brother, as she'd played with her niece. And all he'd been able to think about was how far she'd come. About how a short two years ago she'd been in so much pain that she hadn't even managed to smile at her family.

That Ava was gone.

And because he could see the version of himself from two years ago had disappeared, too— how he no longer feared being hurt, or shied away from his mother's memory—he knew it was time for the next step in their relationship.

He heard her car pull into the driveway and silently thanked his father for giving him the heads-up that she'd left his house. They'd made up some reason for her to take a quick trip to Kirk's after everyone had left. He didn't remember what that reason was now, though that was probably nerves. But because of that made-up reason, he was now ready.

'Honestly, I love your father, but he needs to figure out what's important in life. Particularly at Christmas.'

Noah smiled when she walked in, but his eyes were on Zorro, who'd leapt off the counter and was now searching the kitchen floor for food morsels.

'He asked me all the way back to his house to give me a box of chocolates. *Chocolates.*'

So *that* was what it had been, Noah thought.

'He could have just brought them with him.' She frowned at him. 'What are you doing?'

'I have drinks, popcorn and dessert for a night in.' He walked to her and gently pushed her towards the living room, away from the cat. 'I thought you might want a quiet evening after the busyness of today.'

'Sounds amazing.'

But she didn't sit when she got to the couch—just turned and put her hands on her hips.

'You're acting weird.'

'No.'

He walked back to the kitchen and blocked the cat from darting into the living room. There was a beat when Noah thought Zorro would try again, but then the cat sat down and started licking his leg.

'Something to drink?'

'Noah, you *are* acting weird. Either you tell

me why, or I start the Christmas karaoke up again.'

'Oh, please, *no*.'

Deciding that all he needed for it to be perfect was her, him and the damn cat, he sighed.

'Fine. But I *had* hoped it would go better than this. You and I would be watching our movie. You'd sigh, tell me how I've helped you to love Christmas again, and in would trot Zorro...'

She narrowed her eyes. 'Some of that might happen. But I don't understand—'

She stopped when Noah picked up the cat, her eyes widening as she took in the bow around his neck.

'Oh, he's *festive*.' She walked over to him and took the cat from his hands, just as he'd anticipated she would. 'How did you manage to get him to sit still?'

'I asked very nicely. Told him that if he did I'd legally adopt him.'

'Adopt—'

She broke off as Noah lowered to his knee and her eyes filled. True to who she was, she tried to blink the tears away, but she drew the cat in closer. When Zorro protested, she moved to put him down.

And then she saw the ring.

'*Noah.*'

It was both a gasp and an exhalation of air, and he didn't think he'd ever hear as beautiful a sound again. He took Zorro from her, untied the ring from his neck and gave him a little scratch on the head before letting him go.

True to who *he* was, he ran and hid under the closest table, unimpressed with the past few minutes.

'Ava, you know how much—'

'Noah,' she said again, and her voice was impatient this time. 'I love you, and I'm sure whatever you've planned to say is going to be beautiful, but you can say it to me later, okay? There's only one thing I want to hear right now.'

When he grinned, she shook her head, took the ring from his hand and slid it onto her finger.

'Never mind. I don't even have to hear it. *Yes.* Yes, I will.'

He straightened with a chuckle, but it was cut off when she kissed him. When they pulled apart, she grinned.

'So, how do you feel about wedding planning? Because I vote we get a wedding planner...'

* * * * *

LET'S TALK
Romance

For exclusive extracts, competitions
and special offers, find us online:

f facebook.com/millsandboon

◎ @millsandboonuk

𝕏 @millsandboon

Or get in touch on 0844 844 1351*

For all the latest titles coming soon,
visit millsandboon.co.uk/nextmonth

*Calls cost 7p per minute plus your phone company's price per
minute access charge

Want even more
ROMANCE?

Join our bookclub today!

'Mills & Boon books, the perfect way to escape for an hour or so.'

Miss W. Dyer

'Excellent service, promptly delivered and very good subscription choices.'

Miss A. Pearson

'You get fantastic special offers and the chance to get books before they hit the shops'

Mrs V. Hall

Visit millsandbook.co.uk/Bookclub and save on brand new books.

MILLS & BOON